# Orson Welles of Mars

### A Novel by:

### MAC BOYLE

Party Now.

PN
AL

Apocalypse Later
Industries

Party Now, Apocalypse Later Publishing

A Subsidiary of Party Now, Apocalypse Later Industries

Oklahoma · October Base Epsilon · Iteration 248

This is a work of fiction. Although some historical figures appear within, their actions, behavior, and the events surrounding them are entirely fictitious.

At least, I hope that's the case. It'd be a hell of a time to get this right.

ISBN-13: 978-0692589175
ISBN-10: 0692589171

ALSO BY THE AUTHOR

*Right – A Novel of Politics*
*The Devil Lives in Beverly Hills*
*A Loss for Normalcy*


with Bill Fisher:

*The Adventures of Really Good Man*

For CJ Cregg Boyle
Escape artist, surprisingly skilled veterinarian,
and sniffer of butts.

Of all the souls I have encountered in my travels...
Wait, what's that...?
Stop blabbing and get to the good stuff?

All right, here's your treat.

# PROLOGUE

THURSDAY, OCTOBER 10TH, 1985
2:30 PM PST
ITERATION 343
CBS TELEVISION CITY
LOS ANGELES, CALIFORNIA
EARTH

"Who knows what evil lurks in the hearts of men?"

The production assistant's face sank the instant after he quoted the line. His superiors must have warned against being too familiar with the guest, and the low-level employee now wished beyond his previous capacity to wish that he could somehow replay this event with more wisdom in his arsenal.

Orson Welles spent most of his waking hours lamenting his lack of contribution to human society. He excelled at the activity. When he heard those words, however, he was another man entirely, far removed from the old man who stared back at him in the mirror.

"I beg your pardon?" Welles asked in his default icy tone. In truth, Welles had not ramped up to the fury he produced habitually. The assistant's question was distractingly obscure; that it elicited any memory in Welles was a small miracle.

"They just released tapes of some of your old radio shows. I think *The Shadow* was just the b—"

"Thank you," Welles said. The memory—once hazy—that the assistant tried to elicit focused into sharp relief.

The production assistant dropped the matter. The limits of his time with Orson Welles thankfully precluded further outbursts. "Merv will give you your intro in just a few minutes. He won't bring up anything you haven't already talked about in your pre-interview. Just relax and let Merv do all the work."

Welles did not make eye contact with the production assistant. He refused to take direction from someone too young to have heard his radio performances during their first broadcast.

"Thank you," Welles growled.

"It was a great thrill to meet you, sir," the production assistant tried once more. This time, Welles said nothing. The production assistant knew enough to disappear quietly.

Moments later, the curtain in front of Welles crept open. The studio lighting above nearly blinded him. Welles moved slowly, putting more weight than he liked to on his cane. The damned thing made him appear feebler than he cared to admit. By the time he could discern the silhouette of Merv Griffin, Welles took bold action: He completely removed all weight from his cane and made the last few steps to his host unassisted.

The two men—barely acquaintances—embraced by way of a greeting, affording Welles a moment to lean on the younger man for support. They bantered for a few moments about each other's weight, despite it being Welles' least favorite subject. As that line of inquiry ended, Merv handed Welles a seemingly normal deck of cards, just as it had been prophesied in the fabled pre-interview.

The deck was such a frivolous item to be of interest to anyone, and yet it brought Orson Welles real joy. The crowd too seemed charmed by the sight of such a great man indulging in such an impish grin. Despite the lights being far too bright, a great calm washed over him as he manipulated the individual cards. Sleight of hand was easy. Actual magic would be harder.

$*$     $*$     $*$

"Old age is a *shipwreck*," Welles told Griffin after the commercial break ended. He knew another great man must have uttered those words before, but said man's name remained just beyond his memory. Instead of attempting attribution, Welles emphasized the final word in such a way that the identity of the source he sought might have been none other than Long John Silver.

"But you *feel* wonderful, don't you?" Merv asked.

"Oh, sure," Welles replied, arching his eyebrows to let everyone watching know his true feelings on the matter. His legs were an unending damnation. His jaw had been aching for what felt like several lifetimes. This did not even begin to cover the litany of maladies no longer worth repairing on a model as off-warranty as he. To feel wonderful would have been a fairy tale.

The audience laughed at the playful aside, but then Welles continued. "All these old people who walk around saying they feel just the way they did when they were kids..." Welles lamented. "Liars! Every one of them!"

The old man might have continued, but Merv would not have let the conversation go for as long as it did into the territory of the morose without veering into another *bon mot.* "I just had George Burns on—and he's going to be *ninety*!"

*What the hell does that have to do with* me? Welles wondered before being a good sport about the tangent. "Well, George Burns comes from another planet."

The audience laughed louder than they had at any other point in the interview. It made Welles want to amend the remark with, "No, really..." The moment for an ad-lib passed, and Welles genuinely mourned it. The opportunity to divert the conversation to the topic he truly wanted to discuss might never come again.

"I said to him, and I didn't know how to do it delicately, of course—"

*Liar*, he thought. Merv had built a fortune—too many had done so, in Welles' estimation—upon putting things delicately.

"—I said, 'George, does everything work?'" Merv grinned. It seemed as if he couldn't contain at his own amusement. "He said, 'From the waist up...'"

The audience roared again, even though Merv's delivery was hardly that of George Burns. Welles laughed, too. He had not seen the show, but he could easily imagine Burns making better hay out of the line all the same.

Merv attempted to discuss whether or not Welles was—after everything that had happened to him—a happy person. It was enough for Welles to wish for a meteor to plummet to the earth and end the interview. While most of the country made quick work of reaching for their channel changer, Welles once again attempted to pilot the conversation.

He was not a happy person by nature, and told Merv as much. Yet, he still had the capacity for joyful moments. In 70 years, Orson Welles had encountered unbelievable events, both wonderful and terrible. For every Rita

4

Hayworth, there was a William Randolph Hearst. His acting career, too, afforded extremes of ecstasy and pain, but that seemed like a long time ago.

Like a *maestro* knowing precisely when the concerto needed a dissonant tone, Merv Griffin knew the moment to lean into Welles' dark mood.

"What about the painful times?" Merv asked gently.

"Enough of those to do," Welles remarked. "I'm saving those for *my* book," he added. The crowd laughed again. This time, they were decidedly uneasy in their joy. He doubted he would ever get to write such a volume.

"Were those painful times usually associated with your work?"

*To which "work" would you be referring?* Welles thought, but gritted his teeth together before the words came out.

"All kinds of pain. *All* kinds of pain. Bad conscience pain, too. That's the worst. The times you didn't behave as well as you ought to have. That's the real pain."

Merv relented. He had obtained a confessional interview from Welles, or as close as he would be able to. To go any further might flirt with disaster.

Welles, on the other hand, had been married to disaster for a long time. "You know, Merv. I've been involved in a lot of pain in my life. I've inflicted it. I'm not a very good man. I may never have had the chance to be a better man, but I can't say I tried to be one, either."

"Now, Orson..." Merv said reassuringly. Inwardly, the host was terrified as to where his guest was going with this maudlin monologue. He prayed Welles' depressive state was merely pretense leading to another punch line.

"That needs to change," Welles continued, but he no longer addressed Merv. He spoke to the audience directly. "From this moment on, I will not be responsible for any further bloodshed, and neither should any of you!"

There were no laughs. Merv Griffin's life began to flash before his eyes. The cameras suddenly lost power. The lights in the studio shut off, quickly replaced by emergency lights.

Merv's previous banal pleasantness liquefied in an instant. He leaned in towards Welles. "Are you mad? You'll get us all killed!"

"We're all going to die, Merv," Welles yawned, already fatigued with this *aperitif* to catastrophe. He yearned for the main course. "Some of us much sooner than others."

Merv rose from his seat and addressed the crowd, despite his mind unraveling at the complete hopelessness of his situation. "Ladies and Gentlemen, we're just having some technical difficulties. If you'll stay in you seats, we'll—"

The studio doors burst open. A brigade of men marched into the room and aimed their glowing weapons at Welles. They all wore tight leather garments that reflected the dim remaining lights. A sergeant in a far less imposing tunic and slacks followed behind them.

Several in the crowd cried out in terror. One of the troops fired his weapon into the air. A bright bolt of energy leapt from the gun and eradicated one of the now inactive light fixtures.

Merv moved away from Welles and to the guards. "Gentlemen, I'm sure we can all come to some sort of resolution about this."

They were Merv Griffin's final words. The same guard who destroyed the lighting rig let loose with another volley from his weapon. Merv's eyes went wide an instant before he disappeared entirely. Faint wisps of sulfur filled the studio.

Another explosion of energy propelled the guard back to the other end of the studio. Someone had fired back at him, although the thick armor protected him from any permanent fate.

The sergeant stepped forward. His nostrils flared as he looked to the offender in the studio. The fire could not have come from the audience, nor Merv's crew. As the host's remains dissipated, the sergeant could see Orson Welles. In one hand he held his cane, in the other a weapon identical to his own.

Welles took this opportunity to rise from his seat. He kept his cane close. "Ladies and Gentlemen, there is no need to panic!" Welles said, staring down the barrels of their weapons. "I knew this would happen."

# CHAPTER ONE

SUNDAY, OCTOBER 16TH, 1938
7:27 PM EST
ITERATION 1
CBS RADIO BUILDING
MANHATTAN, NEW YORK
EARTH

One voice rose above all others. It flashed forth from the transmitting towers above and out towards the eagerly awaiting masses.

"The weed of crime bears bitter fruit," the lone voice, 23-year-old Orson Welles intoned as all activity around him stopped. "Crime does not pay! The Shadow knows!"

Orson offered a cackle, inspiring fear in the hearts of evil doers everywhere. Even now, somewhere in the back of Orson's mind, he swore he felt the ground beneath him shake under the impact of his words. Ridiculous though that might have been, it was not likely to deter him from telling people that such a phenomenon occurred.

Despite all of Orson's skills, despite his unquestioned destiny as the master of the airways, another voice usurped his throne. Bills had to be paid.

"And so ends another thrilling adventure of *The Shadow!*" The pretender's voice had no feeling, no pathos, and no theatricality. He was, however, undeniably enthusiastic. The announcer might as well have dragged his fingernails across a chalkboard for all the irritation it brought Orson. "Be sure to tune in next week—"

Orson made his way through the now suddenly active radio studio on one of the top floors of the CBS Building. At a table filled with a menagerie of seemingly unrelated objects, the sound effects foreman consulted the list of tools he needed for the next broadcast. As Orson walked by the table, an idea occurred to him. He might have dismissed the notion as childish, if it wasn't the best idea he had all night.

"And don't forget to burn Blue Coal!" the pretender continued. The second voice belonged to Dan Seymour, whose ambitions had nothing to do with dethroning Orson Welles, Boy Genius. Seymour's one dream began and ended with avoiding a bread line. He might have continued with the advertising copy, but if he hadn't abandoned his post in that instant and dived for the floor, a pound and a half of ground chuck flung from the other side of the room would have slammed against his face.

Seymour slowly rose from the floor, allowing dead air to stand. He could not be certain there would not be another volley from the other end of the studio. However, the show had to go on, even if it was effectively over. Seymour looked beyond his podium and saw Orson Welles standing by the table. The young director had a jar of coins—intended to imitate the sound of shattering glass— in his hands. A malicious grin stretched across his face.

\* \* \*

In the control room, a man watched the familiar scene play out between announcer and predator. He had never fully appreciated the relative safety of a plate glass window separating him from Orson Welles.

"The finest fuel for solid comfort..." Seymour managed to croak out. The announcer could only expel his closing line between fits of flinching orchestrated by Orson.

"All right, everyone!" the technician at the board said as he cut the live feed to the tower. "We're clear!" The technician thought briefly about adding, "Great show everyone!" but as Orson continued to take menacing steps towards Seymour, he opted not to enter the fray.

"They've never been at it this bad, have they?" the technician asked the silent man behind him.

John Houseman said nothing, but instead reached into his jacket pocket for a cigar, and lit the only source of comfort he had left.

"Damned kid..." he muttered as he let the fire take over.

$*$    $*$    $*$

In the studio, only Orson and Seymour remained after the broadcast concluded. Everyone else who might have had reason to be in the room knew all too well of Orson's propensity to create collateral damage.

"It's insipid copy, you Neanderthal!" Orson bellowed.

Seymour tried displaying a strength he didn't actually possess. "I'm not having this discussion with you aga—"

Orson ignored him and continued. "The advertisement is the last part of the program. If your copy is also the worst part of the program, our work is an exercise in futility!"

The control room door swung open, and Seymour took

Orson's slight distraction as an opportunity to beat his own path to the exit.

"It's a miracle you get work at all..." Seymour muttered as he gained speed towards safety.

"What the hell did you just say to me?" Orson quickly grabbed another item off the sound effects table and arced his arm in preparation for the throw of his life. The only item he hadn't already turned into a projectile turned out to be a bag filled with crumpled issues of *The New York Times*. It diminished his menacing stare.

Seymour turned back. "You're 23! I'll say to you whatever I damn well please, you little shit!" he screamed. He only dared the outburst after he knew he could make a hasty exit.

Orson nearly shot the object from his arm regardless of whether or not Seymour was there to greet it. John Houseman now blocked his path. Orson thought better of the attack, but just barely.

"Housey!" Orson cried joyfully, offering up his least believable performance of the evening. He set down the bag of remaindered newspapers.

"Wonder Boy!" Houseman cried back, providing Orson something of a cover by contributing an even less genuine reading of their contrived dialogue.

Orson gritted his teeth as he walked towards Houseman, sending a wave of pain through his jaw. The two men approached each other as the various other workers in the studio felt it was safe to return to their work. Either he was the only man on Earth who could control Orson Welles, or Orson Welles harbored rage for the man more than anyone else he had ever met.

"Well, young man," Houseman droned as he stared Orson down, "how do you feel?"

Orson grabbed Houseman's shoulders. Only Orson

noticed that the other man flinched at the gesture. "I need a drink," Orson barked, released his grip, and then headed for the elevators. "Badly."

Another headache—Orson had long since stopped calling these activities broadcasts—now concluded, Houseman followed his charge.

"Great show, everyone! Keep up the hard work!" Houseman called out to those remaining in the studio. His feeble attempts at peace were somewhat muddled by Orson's left middle finger passing for his own parting words.

$*$  $*$  $*$

Orson entered the elevator first and hit the button for the lobby, not particularly bothered if Houseman was with him or not. The older man managed to enter the car just as the doors closed and the elevator whirred into mechanized life.

The ride to the lobby began in silence, but Houseman took care of that quickly enough. He would never admit it, but peace with Orson was too boring to bear.

"Tough day at the office, honey?" Houseman asked.

"Don't start," Orson warned.

Houseman angrily reached out for the emergency stop button.

"I don't know how many times we have to go through this conversation, but I might as well try once more. There is a Depression on. It has left far too many people out of work. You might have seen them while you race between your numerous sources of employment. And yet, you still work—"

"If I work, you work," Orson corrected.

Houseman's face contorted as if he had eaten a lemon.

Orson's spirit lifted with the rhetorical victory.

"If only we could see a little appreciation from you. Instead, you make it your number one goal to alienate everyone in your path. You'll probably keep on doing so until we're *both* out of work."

Houseman let the words hang in the air as he reached once more for the emergency stop. "Either that, or *you'll* be the one doing advertisements for the rest of your life."

"Commercials?" Orson asked, stricken. "Me? You're out of your mind."

Houseman released the stop, but the car did not move. He flicked the switch again. "Oh, wonderful," Orson groaned. "Trapped in an elevator with you. If the Todd School is beyond these doors and I'm suddenly not wearing any clothes, I'll know I'm still asleep."

Houseman flicked the switch again. This time, a low groaning sound filled the car, as if the wires keeping them at their current elevation were struggling under the weight of the two men. Amidst the grating noise, the lights in the car glowed so intensely that Orson and Houseman felt the need to shield their eyes. After a moment, silence fell again, the light show ceased, and the car moved once more.

"What do you suppose that was?" Orson asked. He didn't believe for a second that Houseman had any sort of faculty to explain what had just happened. However, in the pursuit of any other topic of conversation, Orson would have embraced any number of irrational courses.

"The relays for these new automatic elevators must have overloaded the machinery," Houseman surmised. "If man was intended to fly, God would have let us keep our elevator operators." He smirked at his own *bon mot*.

If Orson had offered so much as a smile, Houseman might have been tempted to release his next piece of information with a little more sympathy. As it was, the revelation felt gleeful.

"There is one more thing, young man. There are a few people waiting for us downstairs."

"Oh God..." Orson lamented when he realized there were no real options for him now other than to suffer through Houseman's trap. He looked over to the elevator panel and only then realized Houseman had pushed a button for an additional floor during his fisticuffs with the emergency stop.

"It's the standard promotional event. We'll be in and out."

The elevator door opened at the third floor, where a secretary stood waiting. She handed Houseman a long swath of billowing black fabric. When she saw the furious terror in Orson's eyes, she immediately ran down the corridor.

"Not the cape and the hat too?" Orson asked. A negative answer was his only hope to elevate Houseman's proposed activity from a living Hell to the rarefied pantheon of abject torture.

Houseman unfurled the fabric and wrapped it around Orson's neck. He placed his own hat on Orson's head. "I'm afraid so."

\*     \*     \*

After they finally reached the lobby, the strength of Orson's indignity increased. Dressed as Lamont Cranston's crime-fighting alter ego The Shadow, Orson stood on display for any gawking simpleton who might walk by. The majority of these slack-jawed oafs consisted of children, nearly brought to tears by the sight of their radio hero brought to life. A velvet rope kept the children at a distance. Such an arrangement was more for the children's safety than Orson's own sanity. Orson's true pain—it had nothing to do with the children—flashed in front of his face.

"Over here, Mr. Welles!" cried one of the photographers.

"Now give us as scary a face as you can, Mr. Welles!"

"Just one more, if you wouldn't mind, Mr. Welles!" shouted another as their bulbs exploded.

Orson hated this kind of light. The flashes were far too bright and intended to blind rather than to illuminate. With the six photographers he could count, the quality of their efforts only served to push him further to the brink of madness.

Orson tried to focus on something—even Houseman's scowling countenance—beyond the photographers. By the time his eyes landed on a background object, his spirit soared, and then immediately crashed.

A cabal of suited men trotted towards the elevators. George Schaefer, President of RKO Pictures, led the group. As a Hollywood chieftain, Schaefer could prove to be one of the few people on Earth capable of lifting Orson Welles out of the endless cycle of hats and capes currently passing for a career.

Knowing his time was brief, Orson tried to find Houseman through the lightning storm that had become his entire field of vision. He saw only red in the wake of the photographers' exposures. For a moment, it felt as if they had ceased their irritating cacophony, as the same strange hum that halted the elevator filled the lobby. Orson attempted to use only his eyes to communicate to Houseman that his patience for this exercise had officially expired. Eventually, Houseman placed himself between Orson and the photographers.

"All right, fellas! Everyone got what they needed?"

Houseman asked, but continued immediately, disinterested in their answers. "Come on now, Mr. Welles is a busy man!"

He shuffled Orson away. "Why did you have me pull you? You don't have to be at the theater for another twenty minutes. You've got plenty of time."

Orson said nothing. His cape fluttered in the rush of air after his sudden movement towards the elevators.

"Mr. Schaefer?" Orson asked in a panicky voice. His anxiety only increased with the extension of a sweaty handshake that the studio head eyed uneasily.

Schaefer's associates exchanged weary glances. He accepted—if hesitantly—Orson's hand.

"Yes, Mr...?"

"Welles, sir. Orson Welles." He regained only the faintest wisp of his confidence. His rebound was not nearly enough to dam the font of perspiration soaking the cloak in front of his face. He suddenly remembered the ridiculous adornment and ripped it off.

"Oh, yes," Schaefer said. "You're the one who directed..." he tried to defer the rest of his memory to his court of associates, but they were of no help. "That Macbeth production, right?"

"Yes! Exactly! It's wonderful to meet you, Mr. Schaefer—"

"Right, right..." Schaefer offered as he turned his attention back to the missing elevator. The contraption was either broken permanently or coming by way of Saturn if there was any accounting for the continued delay.

Orson continued undeterred, having retreated to some far-back section of his brain that could ignore how unimpressive he appeared. "My company, the Mercury Theatre—as you may have heard—is desperately interested in branching out into Motion Pictures. Perhaps we can meet the next time I'm in Los Ang—"

Tragically, the elevator announced its arrival. Schaefer's companions immediately filed in, leaving their leader alone to conclude the encounter with something approaching tact. "Well, we're very busy over at RKO."

"Nice hat," Schaeffer added as the elevator door closed.

Orson only then realized he was still wearing Houseman's fedora. Houseman caught up with his young charge, exacerbating his embarrassment.

"What was that all about?" Houseman asked.

Orson glared at him. In the pulp novels that served only to ruin Orson's life, The Shadow armed himself with two pistols. Now, Orson longed for them. He resigned himself to survive the rest of the evening unarmed.

\*    \*    \*

An ambulance arrived at 485 Madison Avenue several minutes past 7:30 in the evening. After departing the CBS Radio Building, Manhattan traffic attempted to make way for the emergency vehicle while it proceeded northward on 7th Avenue. Unfortunately, the ambulance only managed to reduce its journey by a few scant seconds. Fortunately, with the ambulance's cargo, a few seconds could make all the difference.

Within the vehicle, John Houseman stared at a human form covered by a sheet and wondered if his evening could get any worse. Houseman's companion—a writer by the name of Howard Koch—quietly wondered how he had come to be in the ambulance at all.

"It will take us all of two minutes to get to the theater," Houseman admonished the man under the sheet. "There's no point in trying to fall asleep."

"You never cease to underestimate me," the man on the gurney replied through his shroud.

"That remains to be seen," Houseman countered. "At any rate, if I could trouble you for some attention, Orson. We have business to discuss."

"Fine." With a groan, Orson removed the sheet covering him and sat up.

"Why are we in an ambulance?" Koch asked.

"God!" Orson yelped. He nearly fell off the gurney in shock. "I didn't see you there. Who are you?" Orson turned to Houseman, "Who is he?"

"He's the new writer Virginia hired," Houseman explained to Orson and then turned to Koch. "There is no law that says persons riding in an ambulance must be sick. Sometimes we are in a hurry." Houseman joined his hands together. "Sometimes solutions just present themselves."

"Wait," Orson interjected. "Who's Virginia?"

"Your wife."

Orson smirked. "Oh, yes. Of course. Lovely girl. How is she?"

"Fine," Houseman explained. Further discussion of the topic would only exacerbate the throbbing just inside his temple. "Let's talk about the Hallowe'en show."

Orson grunted and laid back down on the gurney. "Fine. Wonderful. The Hallowe'en show. What are my options?"

"Well," Koch began. He continued only after receiving a reassuring nod from Houseman. "There's *War of the Worlds*. I'm already halfway through the script."

Orson yawned. "I thought I was off comic strip duty for the night. What else?"

Houseman's frown deepened. "Is it simply because the poor boy has already completed work on the project that you find it lacking, or—"

"What *else*, Housey?"

The ambulance turned off its siren and slowed down. Houseman nodded at Koch, but the encouragement hardly helped Koch persevere. "I think I have notes for an adaptation of *Jekyll and Hyde*."

"The New Amsterdam!" the driver cried.

"*Jekyll and Hyde* it is," Orson said as he leapt out of the rear of the vehicle.

"You know if you treated our production schedule with the same care you spend on restaurant reservations, we would be a very great theater company indeed!" Houseman bellowed.

"I don't think he heard you, Mr. Houseman." Koch whispered.

Houseman didn't look at Koch. "It's the only reason I said it."

Koch followed Houseman out of the ambulance. Orson jogged in the direction of the theater, without any consideration for the people he left behind. Houseman seemed either relieved or unimpressed by the snub, as he was already handing the driver an inscrutable amount of folded bills.

"Don't worry about it, friend. Welles is fickle. It is a decent bet he will wake up tomorrow and want to try his hand at *Dracula* again, or maybe even some kind of Lovecraftian nonsense. Here is the best possible solution for all parties involved: Finish *War of the Worlds* but also start work on *Jekyll and Hyde*. We'll pay you for both. Hell, we might even produce both."

The driver looked at the money Houseman handed him and then behind him to make sure Houseman secured the rear door. He put the vehicle into gear and ran his sirens.

Koch shook Houseman's hand before he could alter the deal any further.

"Off you go," Houseman commanded the writer. Once Koch was shuffling back down Seventh Avenue, Houseman considered the New Amsterdam Theatre with a hope and dread competing for his feelings. It was the only type of building that could contain Orson Welles, and Houseman hoped—perhaps with futility—that his evening had finally ended.

*     *     *

Beyond and below the balcony in which John Houseman currently sat, the Mercury Theatre Company presented an early preview of their production of Georg Büchner's *Danton's Death.*

Houseman—and as it appeared by the stifled reaction of the crowd, the audience as well—still had no idea what the play was about. It took place during the French Revolution. That much was clear. However, with its dozens of characters screaming for stage time, Houseman could not fathom anything further. The nebulous quality was likely related to Orson's choice to play nearly two-thirds of the Dickensian *dramatis personae.* Tonight was no less than the seventh time he had seen the play performed in its entirety by the Mercury, and he couldn't be the only one who felt they had a flop on their hands.

Orson was in the middle of a monologue extolling the virtues of liberty. Every word in the cursed script was about liberty, so Houseman could only guess he was listening to a screed on the topic. Orson had not bothered to dwell on the disparity of extolling such noble values, while remaining completely unable to fathom a world that didn't completely submit to his every whim. In a world filled with madmen ruthlessly tearing through the world, Orson may have been tame by comparison. If the man ever got his hands on an army, then "peace in our time" might seem like a far off dream.

As his pontification reached a crescendo, the footlights flared beneath Orson. He made no acknowledgement of the phenomena and carried on as if the electrical problems of the New Amsterdam Theatre responded to his willpower alone. After the lights returned to normal and the chatter from the audience died down, Houseman sensed intruders had entered the balcony and sat near him. He attempted to ignore them until one of them said, "We have a problem, John."

Houseman feigned surprise, but it came out as very genuine annoyance. "Christ, fellas!" he whispered harshly. "Who the hell let you in here, David?"

"We bought tickets," David explained.

"Oh? Well, then. Thank you."

"I was kidding."

"Oh. Well, then. Go to Hell."

"The usher let us in," Davidson Taylor explained. "I represent William S. Paley, the President of the Columbia Broadcasting System, and I tend to get let into a lot of places without being asked for a ticket."

"I know who you represent," Houseman muttered, keeping his eyes forward.

"I heard there was another incident during the broadcast tonight." Taylor continued as if he had Houseman's full attention. Houseman tried to keep his focus on a re-enactment of Bastille Day.

"There's an incident every night."

"Not with an ambulance, there's not."

Houseman finally turned and regarded the other man. "The ambulance took us to the theater."

"Yes, and the last time Welles did that, he tried to have the bill sent to my office!"

A few audience members looked up at the disturbance. Houseman laughed for the first time in weeks.

"I'm usually with him when he tries that little trick," Houseman explained. "And I'm the one who pays off the medic. Sorry."

"Forget the ambulance," Taylor said. "The ambulance is the least of your troubles."

"Indeed."

"The Hallowe'en show is coming," Taylor clarified.

"The Hallowe'en show?" Houseman asked as if he hadn't had a version of this conversation already once this evening. "You mean our normal Sunday cry into the abyss—"

"Don't start."

"No, David. I think I will!" Houseman persisted. "The people have spoken! We could either put together the single most fascinating broadcast since the Sermon on the Mount, or have Wonder Boy down there read the phone book for an hour, and it would not make a difference. The listening public prefers young Mr. McCarthy."

"That's just the problem, John," Taylor interjected.

"That we're getting routinely walloped in the ratings by a radio ventriloquist?" Houseman asked. "Again, we agree."

The audience began a round of applause grounded in the long tradition of polite indifference. In response to such a measured reception, Orson would be an absolute nightmare. That assumed he possessed unrealized potential in behaving boorishly. Houseman took the opportunity to flee the frying pan in favor of the fire and headed out of the theater.

"John," Taylor called after Houseman. "I'm here to tell you, officially, that Orson Welles is more trouble than he's worth."

"Sir, you are positively *filled* with old news tonight,"

Houseman said. He was nearly to the exit.

"John, if the Hallowe'en show doesn't yield a far more substantial audience, the network will have no choice but to pull Mercury Theatre off the air. Mr. Paley wants CBS to be the network for quality programming, but he will not put up with this foolishness forever."

Houseman did not respond, but he had stopped his escape short.

"And without the money we pay you to produce your radio program," Taylor continued, gesturing to include the entire space around him, "The Mercury Theatre itself will be—"

"—finished." Houseman took one moment to glance at the now empty stage with its faux Victor Hugo *mise en scene*. "Well, David, we'll absolutely have to do something about that."

\*     \*     \*

Houseman went back stage without attempting to beg for some sort of reprieve from the network's emissary. For one thing, Taylor seemed to be of a singular mind about the ongoing situation. For another, Houseman was far from empowered to negotiate in these matters. Alternatively, the prospect of Orson Welles' career imploding filled Houseman with a quickly exhilarating and slowly guilt-inducing feeling not unlike a prisoner just emerging from the outer wall of their captivity. This time next month, John Houseman could very well be free of Orson forever. His inner-Orson didn't neglect to remind him that under those circumstances, such a collapse would liberate Houseman from his own income as well.

It would fall on Houseman alone to save Orson from himself. He could only cling to the notion that if he were to rescue the Boy Genius, it would not be for Orson's sake alone.

"Housey!" Orson cried out when he saw the older man emerge from in front of the curtain. Like he had earlier in the evening, Welles grabbed Houseman's shoulders and stared intently at him by way of a greeting.

"My dear friend," Orson said. "Wasn't tonight amazing? Why, at any point during the performance, I felt like I might just fly up off the stage and float off into the heavens."

Joseph Cotton—one of the actors in the Mercury Company—had removed his costume and made his way for the stage door. Genteel in manner, Cotton could not pass either Orson or Houseman without speaking to the two men.

"Good night, John," Cotton said to Houseman, leaving an imperceptible gap before acknowledging the other man with a tentative, "Orson..."

"Hey, Joe!" Orson expelled as he sprang toward the man who was simply trying to go home at the end of a long day. "If one of these nights you're able to get through that monologue in Act II without stepping on the opening line, I'll be the first to go down on you!"

At a loss for either the appropriate comeback or an opportune method to end his indignity, Cotton nodded. "Right, Orson. Maybe tomorrow night will be better."

Orson snarled at Cotton before he disappeared behind the stage door. He then finally noticed the worried countenance on Houseman's face. "What is it, Housey?"

"You're going to Chicago," Houseman replied. He chuckled at the end of the statement, somehow muddling his desire to make the news sound grim.

"No," Orson said, smiling. "*You're* going to Chicago." Another moment passed as Houseman made a concerted effort to keep his face impassive, and Orson's palms grew sweaty. "I don't get the joke."

"You need to take a few days off," Houseman explained. "Go and clear your head for the Hallowe'en show. *Danton's Death* does not get out of previews until November, anyway. This might be the last time you can get out of town for a while."

Orson softened, but almost immediately became suspicious of the appeal to his ego. "Chicago?" he asked.

"Yes."

"Why?"

"I send you to Los Angeles and you will spend all of your time sniffing around every movie studio in town. You will be in a sanitarium before Friday. I send you to Havana, you will bury yourself in your own excess and I will never be able to find you again. If you can think of another location—"

Beyond them, a bulb flashed and then shattered under its own pressure. Glass fell to the ground as Erskine Sanford yelped from fright, and then laughed as the imaginary danger passed. No other lights backstage broke and the ambient illumination around them did not seem diminished.

"If you can think of another location that has any semblance of civilization," Houseman continued. Orson attempted to take this opportunity to be the one to interrupt him, but he was too slow, still dazed as he was by the exploding fixtures. "Anywhere that can both claim to be civilized *and* isn't currently embroiled in a war with fascists, I'll send you there."

Orson thought briefly of Brazil, but then sighed. "Chicago?"

Houseman nodded. "Chicago."

# CHAPTER TWO

Somewhere between the steak dinner for four—one of these days he needed to remember to invite three other people to those events—and the first gust of wind from Lake Michigan, Orson realized Houseman lied to him. Chicago barely qualified as civilized. It was America's answer to the Siberian wasteland, and in three full days of desperate searching, he had yet to find a bartender practiced in the proper construction of a Negroni.

He considered packing and returning to New York as early as Tuesday, but knew he would not hear the end of it if he tried. With Chicago boring him to the point of further self-destruction and a triumphant return to New York out of the question, Orson had no choice but to travel to the last place he was called "Boy Genius" without a trace of contempt or irony.

Woodstock, Illinois, was small—perhaps maddeningly so—and yet filled with enormously fond memories for Orson. He had not lived there in over a decade, and it was only as he crossed the McHenry County line did he realize how much he missed it.

He instructed the beleaguered Chicago cab driver to let him out on the outskirts of town. As he walked along the dirt road that would eventually become Main Street, he entertained the notion that Houseman might have been right. Orson *did* need a break, and the great almost-tundra of the Mid-west was as good a place as any to take one. The wave of nostalgia threatening to overwhelm him reached its crest at the Mercury Diner.

The place was oddly deserted, much like the rest of the town. Only a few years ago the diner would have been bustling with activity. Local teenagers would mill about back then, indulging in any number of frivolous interactions. While they embraced their noxious normality, young Orson Welles—he of the strange Todd School for Boys on the north end of town—sat in a corner table. Those days, patty melts and antique literature provided all the companionship he required. It was in this very greasy spoon that Orson, in the middle of a hamburger sandwich or four, first stumbled upon the notion of connecting much of the Bard's work into a single narrative. The notion that Shakespeare intended his histories to be connected still gnawed at the back of Orson's mind.

Orson entered the restaurant. The smell of burnt coffee nearly knocked Orson backward. A waitress cleaned the far end of the counter, and another younger woman ate at one of the booths. As he sat down at the counter, he wondered if the lack of customers had something to do with the economic woes Houseman accused him of so blithely ignoring. It never occurred to him that the world west of

43rd Street didn't stay open past nine in the evening.

"What'll it be?" the waitress asked, not looking him in the eye. It only made the other customer's persistent gawking at him all the more jarring.

Orson eyed the day's specials scrawled on a chalkboard hanging near the kitchen. He saw the word "rhubarb" and nearly re-thought his plan of attack, before realizing the identity of his dessert was meaningless.

"Slice of pie," he ordered, trying to avoid eye contact with the other customer. "To start."

As the waitress went to retrieve his order, Orson spoke up once more. "Does this place still have a phone in the back?"

The waitress nodded as she slid his pie, a fork, and a napkin on the counter in front of him and then resumed her cleaning. Orson rose from his seat and made his way towards the phone. The woman in the booth still stared at him as if he were the only man in all of the cosmos. The tight, pained expression on his face passed as well. The woman's immovable interest in him could have only one explanation, now that he truly considered the evidence in front of him.

"Hello, yes I am Orson Welles," he confirmed for the woman as he approached her. Her ear flashed bright blue for an instant. Orson immediately dismissed the sight as a stray reflection off of a previously obscured earring. Her eyes went wider after he spoke and removed any remaining doubt that this woman reacted to his celebrity. "I'm not usually one to respond to such atten—"

The woman sprang from the booth and exited the diner without paying. She had not spoken a single word. Bewildered, he took comfort that his embarrassment remained between him and the waitress—who still hadn't looked up from her work—and resumed his path towards the phone.

\*     \*     \*

"I thought the call might have been some kind of joke," the voice of the diner's third customer for the evening called out behind Orson.

"Roger!" Orson cried as he rose from the booth he had commandeered after its previous occupant skipped out on her bill.

The two men embraced. Roger Hill joined Orson at the table. Hill served as headmaster at the Todd School for Boys, that same small boarding school which served as Orson's last stop in the arena of formal education. Despite the length of time since their last meeting, this man remained the closest thing to a family Orson Welles possessed. His own father had been more of stranger than the waitress bringing him pie.

"I should have called sooner. Can you forgive me?"

"Don't give it another thought," Hill demurred. "I'm glad you decided to come see us at all, what with all the excitement you must be experiencing on Broadway. I don't think you've been both west of Philadelphia and east of the San Andreas Fault for close to five years."

Orson's nostrils flared at the mention of his theatrical career. He didn't intend to be hostile towards Hill, but his old teacher must have noticed.

"Excuse me, Miss?" Orson dodged the topic. The waitress approached and Orson hoped he had sufficiently distracted Hill from his line of questioning. "Have something, Roger," Orson insisted.

Hill shook his head. Orson's expectant face insisted Hill reconsider. "Just coffee."

Orson contorted his face in disgust at the timid order.

"I'll have some more pie as well," Orson called after the waitress before she left to grab the coffee.

"We're almost out," the waitress said.

"Then I have my work cut out for me."

Hill looked at Orson after the waitress left. "How are you?"

"Fine."

Hill didn't press, but looked at the four plates on the table. Each had the remains of a pastry that had met an untimely end by Orson's hand.

"What brings you back?" Hill asked.

Orson looked at Hill as if the question were preposterous on its face. "What? I had some time off and could think of nowhere better to spend it."

Hill's eyes narrowed as Orson wondered if his pretense had been too impish for his own good. He was now well past twenty and any behavior once deemed precocious now drifted towards the psychotic. The waitress brought Orson his latest conquest. Some quality of a person's fifth slice of pie in a single sitting made attempts at self-awareness far more difficult to attain.

"I'm stuck."

"Stuck?" Hill asked.

"Yes, stuck." He looked at the new rhubarb with disgust. His stomach had finally turned. This did not limit his ability to take an initial bite. "If anything," he continued after swallowing. "I'm moving backwards. I'm afraid I'm now twenty-three, and my best days are behind me."

Hill looked around frantically.

"What?" Orson asked.

"I'm sorry, Mr. Fitzgerald. I'm a great admirer of your work, but my pupil, Orson Welles just up and vanished right before my eyes."

"Roger..." Orson said. He wanted to protest such a

foolish display, but he hoped Hill had a point.

"It's preposterous," Hill maintained.

"Is it?" Orson asked. The remaining taste of pie in his mouth had become quite bitter. Even he couldn't be compelled to continue with the dessert. "I've done some fine theater, but if I'm an old man and I'm still putting the Roman Army in suits and ties, that's going to be a long life to spend repeating myself.

"I try to move on, but I suppose every man reaches the point in his life when he stops *becoming* the man he's supposed to be and simply *is* the man he always will be."

Hill took a sip of coffee, not displaying the least bit of impatience with Orson's confession.

"It's worse than all that, Roger. Had you asked me two weeks ago if I would be content to just echo through the airwaves for all eternity, I'd have boxed your ears. Now, I'd settle for it. I may have no destiny left to fulfill, and I may soon be out of a job entirely. They're tired of me, Roger. They even had to send me to Chicago, just to be rid of me."

Hill pointed a finger at him, but somehow made the gesture something less than an accusation. "That's just it, Orson," he proclaimed. "You've been worried your best days were behind you since you were seven! You've always wanted to go it alone like some sort of cowboy, but only if everyone is nipping at your heels, desperate to tag along. The moment you reach any sort of resistance you become positively Danish in your melancholy."

Orson tried to move past the comment. "How is the school?"

"Closed nearly three years now." Off of Orson's shocked, silent reaction, Hill continued, "I sent you a letter during our last term."

"I was busy." For the life of him, Orson couldn't recall

Roger's letter or his own schedule at the time.

"I know," Hill said. "That's what I've been trying to tell you, Orson. You were busy then, and you'll be busy again. That's what I hoped I had taught you while you were here. Chase down every opportunity with the talents you have. I guarantee you, no one with your talent has ever peaked at twenty-three."

Orson smiled despite himself. He hoped it wasn't because there was a compliment hidden in Hill's homily. "Thank you," Orson said. In that moment, he made a quiet resolution to return to New York as quickly as he could book a flight. He'd be damned if he would let John Houseman reign over his life a moment longer.

The waitress came by to leave the bill. Hill made a casual reach for it, but Orson quickly grabbed it for himself. There was no further doubt as to Orson's sense of pride, and no doubt that the Mercury Diner had run out of pie.

"The school is gone, but the Headmaster's house still stands. Stay the night with us. The wife would love to see you."

Orson shook his head. The offer tempted, but his newfound determination already had the better of him. "I actually have a..." he began, but then remembered that he had been eating his pie for hours. The cabbie responsible for bringing him here had long since returned to Chicago. There likely wasn't another taxi for dozens of miles, and Orson didn't have the same rapport with Chicago paramedics as he did with their New York counterparts. "Actually, that would be great. Thank you again, Roger. Did you bring the car?"

"Oh, yes, quite so," Hill affirmed. "Are you ready to go?"

The two men rose from the table. "Actually, Roger, do

you mind if I walk the rest of the way?"

"Not at all. Are you sure?"

Orson nodded. "I've got a few things I still need to sort out. I'll be right behind you."

"All right, the light will be on."

\*     \*     \*

As he continued his journey to the old Headmaster's house, the late night air of Woodstock persisted in its quest to rejuvenate Orson. The memories of his time as a boy continued to flood through him. He passed the local newspaper, responsible for publishing his first infuriating theatrical reviews. Further north he could see in the distance the town hall, which served as the center of a festival in the spring. Just after midnight, the hall appeared ghostly in its abandonment. After five minutes of walking, he could see the now empty buildings of the Todd School, only illuminated by the dim lantern of the Headmaster's house.

As he crossed over Main Street, a bronze statue of the town's founder stared westward for eternity. In the spring of 1928, Orson spent a frenetic week tinkering with a play telling the story of the man behind the statue. He eventually thought the townspeople would be bored past tears and straight to the realm of hostility by such a pedestrian tale. In truth, the tale would have thrilled and delighted the town. Orson stopped writing the play because he hated any story where the limits of a man's ambition began and ended in Woodstock.

Hovering just above the statue, a large metal saucer pulsated with green light.

Orson stopped. His nostalgia met its end. He had nearly passed the south corner of Main Street on the way to

Hill's house. Now, he stood perfectly still, taking in the improbable sight. He might have once described such an object as impossible, but that time was a lifetime ago, nearly thirty seconds in total. With no evidence to contradict its existence, Orson Welles had to become accustomed to the reality of an extra-terrestrial flying object. All previous thought he had about the universe became meaningless.

Orson's intellect peeked out from behind his shock to surmise that the craft measured about fifty meters across. Every edge of the ovoid machine was a rounded corner. Random patches of machinery marked the surface of the hull, giving the ship a fragmented, incomplete look. Green energy pulsed from what seemed like the core of the craft and out to the ship's edges. The pus-hued throbbing within the craft appeared to be a byproduct of propulsion. With each wave of the discharge the machine rose and fell relative to the statue directly below.

Orson walked toward the craft. His eyes were wide open, despite the late hour. He feared blinking. The craft might attack, or perhaps disappear altogether. Terror dominated Orson's next moves, and yet he inched closer.

The craft glowed brighter still and lurched forward. This sudden action startled Orson backward onto the hard sidewalk behind him. Sufficiently frightened out of his previous bravery, Orson sprang to his feet and ran for the Headmaster's house. He didn't believe Roger Hill and the former Todd School could protect him, but the open exposure of Main Street was unacceptable.

He rounded the corner, relieved to see the dim light of Hill's house off in the distance. The mere fact that it still existed meant that had Orson gone mad, his psychosis might have only been temporary. It could also mean that the dull world Orson inhabited earlier this evening and the reality he now fought against proved to be one and the same.

He sprinted for the house beyond until suddenly, and as if he were the victim of yet another shock, he fell backward again.

Not understanding—and therefore not acknowledging the existence of—the source of his second stumble, Orson attempted to rise again, but whatever force kept moving him towards the ground was content to keep him there.

An ever-so-slight shift in the light around Orson revealed the shape of a man, or something close to it. As Orson's eyes focused, he saw that the man's head was not a head at all. It appeared to be a solid, spherical orb polished like a sample of black volcanic rock. The man's body hardly qualified as a body either. A thin black fabric throbbed over what might have been the figure's skeleton, but the bones twisted and twirled in unsettling directions.

The man approached, which caused Orson to shift further backwards. "You need to come with us—"

\*　　\*　　\*

And then, there was nothing.

\*　　\*　　\*

But, in the nothing...
PPPPPPPPPPPPPPPPPPPPPREP
ERRRRRRRRRRRRRRRR
FFFFFFFFFFFFFFFFFFFFFFFFFFFFFFFFFFFOR
TTTTTTTTTTTTTR—

\*　　\*　　\*

"*Mr. Welles?*" the voice pierced the nothing, and yet

more nothing remained beyond.

Orson blinked his eyes open. Still on his back, he lay in a drab metal room perhaps twice the size of a telephone booth. The floor underneath and the walls surrounding him resembled the metal of the craft's hull. In its solid uniformity, no other trait of the cell bore further description. Orson could not find the source of the voice piercing the void.

"*Mr. Welles,*" the voice repeated. "*Our vessel is preparing for re-entry. Please prepare for pod ascension and an audience with Chairman Kan-ur.*"

Orson searched for something resembling a door but was unsuccessful. The room moved upward with a lurch, as if it were an elevator. Unable to fathom what indignity lay before him, Orson braced himself against a corner. The ceiling separated above him. One of the walls followed suit shortly thereafter, opening Orson's pod to the area beyond.

The new room had barely more illumination than the unconsciousness from which Orson had just emerged. He saw a dim light at the far end of the chamber, which was the only indication to Orson that this new room was about the size of the entire craft that had taken him.

"Hello?" Orson called out, but received no immediate response.

"George Orson Welles. Born May 6, 1915, in Kensoha, Wisconsin, to the late Richard Hodgdon Head Welles and Beatrice Welles, née Ives. Spouse Virginia Nicholson, currently estranged. One daughter named Christopher. Current position: Director of the Mercury Theatre Company and star of *The Shadow*, presented by Blue Co—"

"That'd be me," Orson interrupted as he approached the source of the light. The same figure that loomed over him on the road to Hill's house stood over the lit panel. "I believe you have me at a disadvantage, sir." Was the figure in front of him even a "sir"? The voice sounded masculine, but no other feature assisted with Orson's understanding.

"Re-entry will be complete in twenty seconds," the voice that awoke Orson called out from all directions. The shape then placed his hand on the glowing panel just ahead. With a faint mechanical noise as a response, the darkness surrounding Orson and the shape suddenly disappeared. In its place was a bright red fire displayed on every wall around Orson and his alien captor.

The new sight activated a deep but brief flash of pain within Orson's eye sockets. The illumination did make the strange figure in front of him clear for the first time. The clarity did not ease Orson's apprehension about him, as the figure appeared to possess roughly the same features in both the light and the shadow. The film-like skin or fabric still pulsated around an improbable skeletal structure, and the polished orb in lieu of a head appeared no more human. Something fluttered within the figure's skull. The movement might have been some sign of life, although it certainly did not give the shape anything approaching a human quality.

"I am Kan-ur," the figure spoke. "And to answer your next question, Mr. Welles, you are not being held. You are my guest. I have invited you here because events have escalated and it is far too dangerous to leave you on your own."

"That's not *much* of an answer," Orson spat as he approached closer. He wasn't sure if he was more upset about the kidnapping, or that this strange creature viewed Blue Coal as worthy of his C.V. Before he sorted through the plethora of follow-up questions racing through his mind, the view around them changed once more. The fire disappeared, and the ocean remained.

The coast of the far off land and the water that nestled

it looked pale, even sickly. If this place once nourished life, then that life had long since ceased supporting the place. Symbiosis had ceased, and only a feeding parasite remained. Large buildings speckled the coastline, spewing cyclones of dark, black smoke that drained the environment of its remaining color. Small flecks swarmed above the surface, like gnats near recently spoiled food. As their ship approached the surface and passed the thickest layers of industrial smoke, the pests appeared to be automobiles soaring back and forth in the sky above the alien city.

From this vantage, everything was clearer. Orson could see a mural of graffiti on one of the large, smoke-belching buildings. It read in bright, red paint:

#octobersurvives

The mark served only to further Orson's confusion. The vista was so spectacularly alien, and yet still so familiar, right down to the pseudo-English of the graffiti. Orson's mind struggled to grasp what he had seen since he left the diner, but every subsequent development seemed to contradict the one it succeeded.

"What is this place?" Orson asked.

"Took you long enough," Kan-ur said. His tone sounded sardonic, if Orson allowed for the possibility that a creature such as Kan-ur was capable of sardonicism. "Mr. Welles, you've come home. We are approaching the island of Manhattan."

Orson feared he was having a stroke, or in throes of some other fatal phenomenon on that street in Woodstock. Death didn't come with a flash of pain. Life truly ends in a series of absurdities as the synapses of the brain slowly collapse. Regardless of whether or not he was still alive, Orson took a step forward and considered the sight of the strange, corrupted New York before him.

"Welcome to the future, Mr. Welles," Kan-ur said. "Welcome to the year 2000."

# CHAPTER THREE

SUNDAY, OCTOBER 15, 2000
2:35 PM EST
ITERATION 343
MANHATTAN, NEW YORK
EARTH

Kan-ur's craft landed on a large platform jutting out of a building on the east end of Broadway. In truth, Orson could only estimate his location. To believe the story as Kan-ur told it, Orson might have landed back at the site of the New Amsterdam Theatre sometime after his eighty-fifth birthday.

At the far end of the cavernous control room, a large section of the wall opened up to let in a column of hazy light. Three shadows approached, eventually clarifying into the image of three men. Each wore garments made of the same black fabric that draped Kan-ur's body, but theirs were augmented with sections of harder plastic covering their joints.

The newcomers appeared more human than Kan-ur as well. The skin exposed on their faces had the pallor of

Chaplin's Little Tramp, but the presence of any face provided some comfort. Each of the men had long hair draped down to their shoulders, and the weapons they carried appeared to be a cross between a prop from an adventure serial and an object of actual lethality.

"I thought they were supposed to be kept outside the city borders while the operation was underway," Kan-ur complained to the three men as the craft powered down around them.

Two of the guards persisted in staring at Orson. The third guard occasionally glanced in his direction.

"Only one of their squads broke through, Commander. We have them pinned down now around Princ—"

"But they were allowed to make their mark on the Western power plant?" Kan-ur's arm flitted in the direction of the grafitti'd building in question. "October *survives*? Unacceptable, gentlemen."

The guards exchanged uneasy looks. "There were several attacks this time, sir..."

"What? What could you mean? They barely have the resources to buy the spray paint!"

"There are reports that they have a base camp near the Olympus facility or at least on the surface of the planet in one of the unpopulated areas. They may have—"

"They may have what?" The machinery within Kan-ur's frame whirred against the stress of his tone.

"They may have sent a team through the arch," the third man said.

Although it was difficult to tell with his lack of features, Orson got the sense that Kan-ur was now staring at him as well. "Take him away," Kan-ur barked to his guards. "I will clean up your mess myself."

Before Orson could offer a word in protest, the three men ushered him off the top deck of the impossible ship and out into the world. As he moved away from the ship and into the open air, Orson saw Kan-ur reactivate his vessel and float into the sickly heavens beyond.

*   *   *

The differences between the future and the past struck Orson far more than the similarities. Streets as he had encountered them previously no longer existed, as the vast expanse of the island now appeared to be covered pedestrian walkways made of the same smooth, dark metal that made up Kan-ur's ship. The flying cars zooming above his head hardly seemed any more efficient than the antiques driven by Orson's contemporaries. The new vehicles were slower than an ambulance. Orson could be sure of that much.

The similarities did not escape him, either. Orson had to see the future in sharp relief to realize that his home, the world of 1938, had little to offer the eye beyond a wonderland of printed advertisement. Antiquity had the Globe Theatre, the Coliseum and Stonehenge. The twentieth century answered these aesthetic wonders with boxing matches, chocolate bars, and vaguely disquieting propaganda handbills preparing for a war of which the populace insisted they wanted no part. Two full millennia since the birth of Christ, humanity had not re-embraced their potential for beauty. Progress in the year 2000 merely forced the advertisements to shift constantly. Not one message stayed in position on the myriad flat panels of glass for longer than a few seconds. The whole of society appeared to suffer from a perpetual identity crisis. The impermanence of Orson's surroundings might have possessed a Buddhist quality, if it weren't so irritating.

The air felt heavy, but tasted sweet. Orson spent the

first several minutes enjoying it as the flavor was reminiscent of the flavor in Dr. Pepper, but immediately became a frightening sign that something wrong, perhaps even evil, filled the air around him.

The guards and Orson passed by a large plaza. Concrete chairs precisely arranged over the surface of the vista made the area look like a graveyard. Wires trailed out of the ears of each throne occupant, leading to a nearby mechanical apparatus. The devices glowed with the same hue and intensity as Kan-ur's flying saucer, but all of the machines focused their discharge directly into the attached people. Each face contorted into a tight grimace, and yet their eyes showed no reaction to their stimuli at all. Orson hadn't seen this many people so sedated since the last time Olivier performed at the Phoenix.

"What are you doing to those people?" Orson asked. He attempted to move closer to the stricken mob, but one of the guards restrained him.

"They don't have schools in your time?" the guard asked as they now moved Orson even faster along the street. If Orson didn't look directly in front of him, he would likely fall to the harsh metal ground.

Against all probability, some buildings around them Orson did recognize, although scorch marks painted the surface of each structure. Their existence pointed to two still inconclusive truths. First, Kan-ur's assertion that Orson was now in his own future might be true, and second, the world saw an unfortunate level of strife in the years between Orson's home and this sickly-sweet cacophony.

They eventually entered one of the modern skyscrapers. The air within was cleaner, if a bit cool for Orson's immediate comfort. The guards led him into an elevator. Once the doors closed, the car shot up suddenly, forcing Orson's ears to pop painfully.

Once they arrived at their destination, Orson saw a long metal hallway. The guards pushed him through the entry at the other end of the passage and into a large, furnished apartment.

"What am I supposed—" Orson yelped, but saved his energy when he heard a lock click behind him.

*     *     *

The world seemed smaller, but no less unfamiliar from the safe vantage point of the penthouse. Orson spent a long time looking out the windows facing north, trying to get a better sense of his surroundings. It appeared he was on the south end of Manhattan. No other building approached the height of his current vantage point.

After it became clear that his captors intended to leave him to stew in these accommodations indefinitely, Orson explored his more immediate surroundings. The same glowing rectangles that so unnerved Orson on the streets below sprang up like weeds in the penthouse. For a solid hour, Orson eyed a smaller version of one of the contraptions as data and images filled its screen.

An aircraft—larger than the cars Orson had previously seen—buzzed the penthouse and interrupted his fascination. The craft made a terrible racket and spewed smoke from its tail. Other craft—police, judging by their blinking blue and red lights—met the fuming glider and vaporized it in an instant.

It was only after the fireball wreck of the aircraft impacted with the ground that Orson realized the plane had written a message in the sky with its exhaust, it read:

#octobersurvives

The fate of the authorial aircraft weighed heavily on Orson as he got the sinking feeling that they intended their dying message for him. He wondered if a society able to access all human knowledge in an instant doomed itself to produce people who thought they were the central figure of every event that occurred around them. While this feeling of solipsistic guilt didn't ebb with his theory of inevitability, Orson couldn't avoid the glowing glass rectangles for long. The machines' insidious lure knew no bounds.

After trying to reposition one of the devices, Orson only then realized one could manipulate the information displayed by touching its glass surface. Orson wondered why the designers of the future arranged characters on the input screen exactly like a typewriter. The scourge of stuck hammers had to be the dominion of antiquity. Having now mastered the device's fluid, yet rudimentary control mechanism, Orson attempted to find any sort of news pertaining to the downed aircraft outside his window. His efforts were fruitless.

His mind wandered to more general information about the future. He typed in "Present Day Los Angeles." The computer returned nothing close to the information Orson sought. Grimacing, he surmised his supposed mastery of the machine was far less than he initially measured.

The siren song of his true curiosity proved too much to bear. He looked over his shoulder, although he wasn't sure why he did so. If Kan-ur's forces had him under surveillance, the temptation Orson currently nursed couldn't have been more of a breach of decorum than his previous queries.

He typed "Orson Welles" into the computer.

The machine displayed nothing in response. No cacophony of unhelpful tangents, or ads for marital aids.

Orson's screen displayed no information whatsoever.

Positing that he could only obtain the correct information with as detailed a query as possible, he typed "Orson Welles biography" across the glass surface.

Again, nothing. If Orson could have imagined an inanimate object capable of such a reaction, he would have thought the machine was equally surprised.

He felt a gnawing pain at the pit of his stomach as he typed "Orson Welles Date of Death".

The machine produced an almost insectoid clicking in its struggle, displayed an ominous bright blue screen, and then blinked off entirely. Orson's frustration at the computer's insistence he never existed eased only when the contraption took mercy on him before revealing such a grim piece of trivia.

He explored the rest of the apartment, and delighted in two discoveries in particular. First, a wardrobe filled with garments in various sizes made of the ubiquitous black material now fashionable. Second, humanity had not changed so drastically in the intervening years. The water closet still possessed recognizable features.

He washed and traded in his clothes for one of the garments. Depending on one's perspective, he hadn't changed clothes in 62 years. The new material had all the aesthetic and tactile pleasures of a rubber hose, with only marginally more flexibility. As he washed his face and looked into the mirror, he reached for the pockets of his now ancient clothes. He found his pipe, and an unopened package of tobacco. Tamping the leaves into the pipe's chamber soothed him, whether from the joy of engaging in an activity he understood, or the release of endorphins in anticipation of the impending smoke. He dug further in his clothes and found a matchbook. Flicking his thumb across the top of the stick, the air around Orson thinned sharply.

The flame settled, and he attempted to light the tobacco.

"Please don't do that!" a voice called out from the ether.

Orson dropped the pipe from his mouth as the match exhausted itself. Panic bubbled through his body as he saw an additional figure staring out of the mirror back at him.

Orson whipped around, but he was still alone in the small room. Calming down significantly, but with his heart still pounding in his chest, he looked once again in the glass. The reflected figure appeared translucent and amorphous. Orson had a difficult time focusing on any particular feature of the phantom. Obscured as it was, the body was only a sketch of a normal man's frame. The neutrality of the face made it appear as if a sheet covered it. It grinned vapidly at Orson. Orson went silently through a checklist of new experiences that now included flying saucers, travels across the fourth dimension, glowing rectangles everywhere he looked, and now ghosts before he finally said, "Hello?"

"Hi there!" the ghost yelled, startling Orson back against the wall. "I'm Schmoogle Boogle, your friendly digital assistant! I'm afraid I can't allow consumption of tobacco."

"I beg your pardon?" Orson reached for the pipe on the ground. He put it back in his mouth.

The figure in the mirror went red. Two panels on the mirror slid open. Nozzles emerged from the holes and shot bright blue electricity in Orson's direction. He dropped the pipe again in a convulsion and opted not to pick it up again.

"Tobacco products can prove deadly to your person, the people around you, and the environment. It's strictly forbidden, but you should know that!"

"And now I gaze upon the face of Lucifer..." Orson

lamented.

"Now, how can I help you today?"

"What?"

"I don't understand the question!" the specter replied. The being seemed positively tickled by its own confusion.

"How are you speaking to me?" Orson asked, and then rolled his eyes at the absurdity of... well, everything at this point. The feeling did not abate as the emanation's face suffered some sort of a fit and distorted in response to the question. It resembled the surface of a pond, and Orson's question skipped across its surface like a rock.

The blur lifted and the "assistant"—as that was how it identified—looked straight at Orson. "Years ago, the Schmoogle Boogle Corporation developed the first thinking, self-aware computer. The practical applications of such technology were not—as most people assumed—for the purposes of war and destruction, but for three main purposes." A bell rang off in the distance. "First, connect average citizens faster than ever before." The bell rang again. "Second, bring people all the information they would ever need." The bell started ringing non-stop now. "And, last but not least: make their lives much easier. Remember, we're Schmoogle Boogle! We're here to help you, not kill you!"

A smile spread across Schmoogle Boogle's face as the ringing stopped and the bathroom filled with the far off sound of an unseen crowd laughing politely.

Orson approached the mirror to ask more questions, but S.B.—for so it will be convenient to speak of him— slammed its hand against its side of the mirror. The action produced a loud noise, but did not appear to shake the glass.

"Want to learn more?" S.B. asked. Orson kept his distance, feeling like a dog assessing the threat of an unknown human offering a piece of bacon. "Just place your hand here!"

Orson moved closer to the mirror. The glass was warm, and the instant Orson touched the projection of S.B.'s hand, its entire figure flashed green an instant before turning bright red.

"I'm sorry," S.B. lamented as his normal, phantasmagorical complexion returned. "But your account has been suspended!"

Orson swore S.B. now eyed him suspiciously, despite that being roughly akin to an icebox proposing marriage. "Would you like to make another sign-in attempt?"

Curious more than confused now, Orson connected his hand to S.B.'s once again. The phantom in the mirror turned green and then instantly red once more. This time, S.B.'s furious crimson complexion lasted longer. His face twisted and contorted once more as well.

"I'm sorry! I have no log in information under that handprint information. Would you like to try again or continue to surf the network's basic information?"

Orson slammed his fists against the bathroom counter. S.B. neglected to react to the outburst. In the quiet that followed, Orson mulled asking again for the answer denied him previously, but opted for the one for which he was sure he wanted an answer.

"What does the world look like beyond New York?" Orson asked without looking up at the machine.

S.B. didn't even bother with the mechanized equivalent of contemplation. "I don't understand the question!"

"Los Angeles, London, Madrid, Wisconsin?" Orson barked. "Show me what they look like now."

"I'm sorry. I have access to no images beyond the furthermost borders of Manhattan."

"That doesn't mean they don't exist..." Orson's eyes

narrowed.

"I'm sorry, I can't hear you!" S.B. crooned. "Is there something else with which I can help you?"

Orson dropped to the floor, desperate to see some sign of the mechanism bringing this Pepper's Ghost to the washroom. Aside from the polished stone of the fixtures, he saw nothing. The specter did not come from any projector or any other type of technology as Orson previously understood it. Whatever this creature was, it lived inside of the mirror.

He slowly backed towards the washroom's exit. He kept his eye on the phantasm just as it continued to eye him.

"No, thank you," he told the ghost in the toilet mirror.

"Very well. Can I interest you in some nice pornography? There's always plenty of pornography!"

"No," Orson maintained as he made his way out of the room as quickly as he could. All the while as he made his escape, a potent and sudden fear consumed him. If the search engine required a hand print to access most of its available information, Orson shuddered to fathom what sort of contact would be required to obtain the other information it offered.

Orson entered the living room. S.B. stood near the window, free of the bathroom mirror and perpetuating his vacant grin. The mechanized ghost appeared nearly solid in front of him, then disappeared and reappeared at several other spots in the room.

Orson grumbled irritation at S.B.'s persistence.

"I can also offer you an extensive list of programs to watch! The entire new season of 'Frozen Peas' is available right away, if you'd like."

Orson attempted to stand still and let S.B. convulse like lightning around him. How did humanity build these great and terrible cities, while at the same time suffering an unending series of interruptions?

"Leave me alone!" Orson growled.

"I'm sorry. There aren't any lending banks nearby. Shall I try searching the net for one?"

"I don't understand anything you're saying!" Orson felt a spasm in his eyelid. "And I *hate* that!"

Both entities were ripped from their conversation suddenly, frightened out of their focus by a buzzing noise filling the apartment. Orson briefly wondered if it was another aircraft attempting a strafing run for the building, but the klaxon was too brief and he saw no sign of disturbance beyond the window. It was only when the noise occurred a second time that he surmised the harsh, mechanical sound was what passed for a door chime in the future.

Orson went to the front door and opened it with great hesitation. Beyond the door was a sight so comforting, so perfectly familiar, that Orson could not help but sigh with relief. Halfway down the hallway to the elevator, a bellhop pushed a dumbwaiter populated with alluring covered dishes towards Orson. The food could easily have been terrible, but it smelled like food, and set Orson's imagination aflame. The sight of Kan-ur in front of the feast only marginally diminished Orson's enthusiasm.

Kan-ur politely stood still, waiting for Orson to decide what he wanted to do about the meal. Orson let the food in.

"Mr. Welles," Kan-ur began once it was just the two of them in the corridor. "My profound apologies for leaving you when I did. I am sure you have many questions for me," he gestured with his thin arms toward the door separating them. "May I join you while you eat your meal?"

Orson flinched. Schmoogle Boogle floated a few feet

behind him.

"Hi there! I've got several restaurants nearby, many of which offer delivery!" the spirit offered to anyone who would listen.

"Computer off," Kan-ur ordered. The entity made a sour face and promptly disappeared.

Orson ultimately supposed that despite Kan-ur's courtly manners, his degree of choice in letting him enter might be an illusion. Besides, if the chairman proved able to get rid of the cloyingly helpful S.B., he may be Orson's only hope to weather the oddities of the future. He gestured for the orb-headed figure to enter.

\*     \*     \*

The food proved as tasty as it smelled, although that may have been a byproduct of Orson's extreme hunger. Between mouthfuls of some manner of stew, Orson eyed his guest. Kan-ur neglected to eat anything, nearly to the point of rudeness. Orson eventually realized Kan-ur's polished face and the rest of his anatomy lacked an avenue for ingestion. When Orson had enough food to effectively combat a headache that travelled with him through the ages, he finally spoke.

"I do have one question above all others," Orson confessed.

"How did a man with a connection to our computers get into your bathroom mirror?" Kan-ur tried to pose the question for Orson so that he could continue eating but the man had moved past his stew.

"Two questions, then. The *main* question I have is: Why?"

"More specifically?" Kan-ur asked in a tone that was still too mechanical and ethereal to be amused.

"Why me? Why here? Why now?"

Kan-ur leaned forward. Under other circumstances, one might have assumed he was going to take a bite of food in order to delay an answer, but he must have been merely contemplating his next words.

"So you accept that we have not left your home planet, but propelled years into your own future?"

"I allow that there is plenty of evidence to support, if not prove that assertion, yes. First, there are a number of buildings I recognize that have—after a fashion—survived. Second, everyone—and everything—here is speaking something akin to English as opposed to some sort of Venusian or Saturnian dialect. I'm supremely positive that if we were somewhere beyond the stars that you wouldn't be the most inhuman individual I've encountered, nor would your underlings speak the language of Shakespeare."

Orson worried for a flash that the word "inhuman" may be taken as an insult. Kan-ur showed no reaction to the remark at all. "And third?"

"I didn't say that there were three things that influenced my thinking."

"Regardless, I have a feeling that there is a third."

Kan-ur was correct. Orson pointed out the window covering the wall to his left and into the darkening sky beyond. "That moon bears a certain resemblance to a lunar body of my youth, but what's more the stars are exactly the same. Obscured, certainly by the haze that permeates everything, but still the same sky. No matter what strange things you might show me, sir, the sky does not lie."

Kan-ur softly applauded the reasoning. The sound of his appendages slapping together sounded less like clapping and more like someone shuffling sheets of paper together.

"Well done, my friend," Kan-ur said.

"You still haven't answered my question," Orson said

coolly.

"Indeed." Kan-ur rose from his seat at the table and moved over to the tablet of black glass Orson had spent most of the afternoon trying to master. "I had some concern we would have to go over the basics. 'Why *is* everyone speaking English?', 'Is this a dream?', et cetera—"

"I'm not convinced this isn't a dream," Orson countered.

Kan-ur deftly manipulated the controls of the device with his improbable arms. The glossy, bright images of the news and weather blinked away in favor of bright purple text that reminded Orson of indecipherable mathematical discourse written on blackboards in the background of photos of Albert Einstein. Kan-ur, while making these changes to the device, managed to make a noise that resembled a hydraulic valve releasing. It may have been what passed for a reproachful sigh with him.

"Come now, Mr. Welles, you of all people can appreciate the impermanence of dreams. Are your surroundings not fundamentally consistent? And why haven't you awoken?"

The image of S.B. briefly flashed into existence in the front of the room, not as a specter in the bathroom mirror, but as a full floating projection phantasm possessing the same claim to dimension as Orson and Kan-ur. The digital assistant appeared furious at being disturbed, but disappeared as rapidly as he came to life. A projection of a globe replaced him.

"This is the earth as you left it," Kan-ur explained. "Now, a simple fact of humanity's existence is that after a certain point of technological development, the earth's resources will begin to ebb. It is... Well, *some* say it is inevitable. I am possessed of a different viewpoint."

He manipulated the controls further and the image of

the Earth grew dim, with the oceans adopting a greyish tint, and the landmasses hued brown. A number floating above the globe's projection switched from "1938" to "2000." He manipulated the controls once more and the seas became black, with the land a dark grey. The image now resembled the beginning of a Universal Picture. The time display satellite shifted to "2184".

Orson nearly formed a question for Kan-ur, but the alien continued his presentation. "Eventually, your people's short-sightedness will be your undoing."

The image of the Earth disappeared. More appropriately, it shrank and glowed red. "Humanity then moved to the Earth's nearest cousin and attempted to carve out a new life. This is how I found your people."

The ship Orson first saw back in Woodstock blinked into existence orbiting Mars.

"Humanity's suffering was overwhelming then," Kan-ur explained as the image shifted to Kan-ur overlooking a throng of dirty, ragged, and ultimately miserable humans packed into a large dome on the surface of the red planet.

"I could not allow such a once great people to come to a miserable end. I had the ability to fix your fate. I had to try."

The image shifted once again to that of an armada of ships similar to Kan-ur's moving between the red orb and the grey Universal logo.

"In addition to being able to travel among the stars, my people developed the ability to travel through the fourth dimension, just as your H.G. Wells could only imagine."

As the crafts sped up, there was a bright flash. When it cleared, the caravan arrived at a brand new green-blue globe, and the calendar showed "1938" once more.

"I brought humanity back to what it once was. I brought them to live in perfect peace alongside their ancestors," Kan-ur explained.

Orson quietly wiped his mouth and placed his napkin on the table. "You made all of humanity—in the future—refugees in their own past."

Kan-ur extended his arms. "I couldn't have said it better myself."

Kan-ur prepared to elaborate further, Orson still had more specific issues to clarify. "What makes you think humanity will do any better with a second chance at the Earth?"

Kan-ur said nothing, and instead turned off the three-dimensional projector. "I hoped they would. I truly did. You can see for yourself that the world is already souring under the continued progress of civilization. This is why we have to try again."

"Again?" Orson asked. His confusion felt all the more frustrating as he believed he followed Kan-ur's Rube Goldberg machinations up until then.

"We start the process over again: transport all of human society to the same point—your home, 1938—so that humanity can have a *third* chance." Kan-ur sounded more human than he had at any point previously. Orson tried not to dwell on the realization that Kan-ur also never sounded more insane.

"How do you avoid running into yourself doing it the first time?" Orson entertained Kan-ur's story merely because the realities around him lent credibility to the fantastic.

"You're thinking of time in a linear fashion," Kan-ur admonished Orson, and yet there was only minimal movement in his body as he did so. "Each time we travel back we create a different alternate reality, free of the constraints, pain, or mistakes of the one that came before. Humanity can have as many fresh starts as it needs."

"It's incredible," Orson admitted. "And yet-"

"I knew it," Kan-ur said, slapping his appendages on the table. "I knew you would understand. I had a very good feeling-"

"There is still much that confuses me," Orson interrupted Kan-ur, although he immediately wondered if that was the wisest course. "And you still haven't answered the most pressing question."

"Which is?"

"Why me?"

Kan-ur offered that sharp hiss of his once more. "You must have sensed it. I've made it my life's work to ensure humanity has a future, but I cannot be the face of that future. I'm too dissimilar..." Kan-ur said nothing for several seconds, nor were there any wisps of sound coming from him. For a moment, Orson wondered if some malady had befallen the man. Kan-ur eventually reclaimed his train of thought. "I need a voice for the future, Mr. Welles— Orson—a partner, and I can think of no one better suited either here in the year 2000 or in 1938, to get the job done. Will you help me, my friend?"

Orson looked down at his food. Convinced that the dish was now cold and without flavor, Orson's mind wandered to a brief vision of himself standing next to Kan-ur, explaining to his contemporaries their role in the salvation of mankind. He had one additional question. It was a query he tried with all of his available self-control to stifle.

"Who is October?" Orson asked as he felt that control slip away from him.

Orson could not mistake the sudden stiffening of Kan-ur's frame as anything other than the introduction of a difficult subject. "He was someone very important to the people of Earth. He's no longer with us. He was a good friend in his time."

"But why do those markings and the skywriting say—"

Kan-ur slammed his arms on the table. The sound was less resonant than if Orson had committed the action himself, but it surprised nonetheless. It was as if his hands suddenly developed more heft in the midst of the angry outburst.

"—because they lie!" The words warbled as they left Kan-ur's spherical skull.

Silence filled the room, aside from the tinny whine of the dishes still vibrating in the wake of the outburst. Kan-ur gestured—Orson assumed snapping was outside of his available skills—for the bell hop to approach from the kitchen area to take the remainder of the meal away. The bell hop moved with frightened, nervous speed that did not diminish his efficiency. He did not stay long enough to solicit a tip, and Kan-ur was almost immediately behind him.

"But I have more questions—" Orson called after him.

"Please wait here until I call for you again," Kan-ur said abruptly. Orson followed the mysterious figure to the apartment door in an attempt to sue for more information.

Kan-ur offered nothing further as he exited out into the corridor, and closed the door behind him. After the door made an additional clank Orson suddenly remembered that, despite Kan-ur's flattering entreaties, the door to the penthouse only locked from the outside.

# INTERLUDE

THURSDAY, JANUARY 4, 2210
9:03 AM COORDINATED MARTIAN TIME
ITERATION 1
OLYMPUS INSTITUTE
OLYMPUS MONS, MARS

"When I said we're open to any idea, no matter how ridiculous, perhaps I should have clarified." The Chair of the Institute eyed the stopwatch on her tablet, desperately hoping that her interruption would push her past the two-minute time limit she had instituted.

The Scientist who currently had the floor attempted to regain his control over the proceedings. "I'm completely serious."

"Time travel?" the Chairwoman's Chief Aide interjected. In the time he could have used to pursue serious work, the Aide instead spent his entire career redefining the word obsequious with every successive action. "What will we use to accomplish this task? A flux capacitor? Or perhaps you suggest we take a page from Mark Twain. We'll fall asleep under a shady tree and when we awake it will be at a time when the Earth is green and plentiful!"

At the conference table carved out of Martian rock, a few of the other scientists laughed at the remark. The Chairwoman smirked, which only made her immediately subsequent disapproval sharper. Even she couldn't see a future where her closest advisor could succeed her as leader of the Institute.

While he still held the floor, the Scientist persisted in his point. "We all here know it's possible. While we wouldn't be able to travel with any sort of precision or accuracy, the mechanics of a temporary Einstein-Rosen b—"

"Are still quite theoretical!" the Chairwoman interceded once again. "Even if a wormhole in space-time *were* a question of engineering and not theoretical physics, the power needed to generate such a doorway—"

"We have decades of data on a litany of high-energy phenomena in the space between us and the old planet!" the Scientist blurted out before he could have any sort of opportunity to consider the impact of his words.

"Energy that we can both predict and harness didn't exist on Earth and it certainly is beyond our means presently. My predecessor founded the Olympus Institute as a beacon of hope for hopeless people. We are charged with using the latest technology to ensure humanity's future, not to wander through fruitless discussions of the purely hypothetical. This course of action is no more scientifically sound than petitioning a God to deliver us from our self-destruction in a fit of mercy it never saw clear to exercise before. We need plans, sir, and not foolish dreams."

The conference room simmered in silence for an excruciating stretch. To break the icy vacuum that now surrounded the Olympus board, the Aide cleared his throat. "What about the October Archive?"

"The October Archive is a *myth*," the Scientist hissed. He also would never have guessed that the Aide would present an idea even more outlandish than his own. "You might as well suggest we transmit a message into the cosmos and hope that a benevolent extra-terrestrial provides us with a sustainable livelihood."

"Both have just as much, if not more, of a chance of success as your... *suggestion*," the Chairwoman stated. Her face did not appear to give way to any further negotiation on the matter. The Scientist offered nothing further in his own defense and watched as the Chairwoman took his statement about the Archive as a conclusion.

She acknowledged one of their other colleagues. He proceeded to offer a suggestion involving more aggressive terraforming of the Martian surface. What the suggestion possessed in plausibility, it more than made up for in its weakness. The discussion evolved into brainstorming a potential plan to re-terraform Earth. No one mentioned the atmosphere of their home planet was so aggressively toxic that such a plan would be as useless as anything else provided. They'd have an easier time trying to homestead the Sun. The Scientist considered mentioning these objections, but didn't follow through. He figured they would come to that conclusion on their own.

Another member of the board then proffered a presentation of the latest estimates on continued resources. The Scientist had already read his emails. He knew the data. Inside of 100 years, Mars would be as dead as the Earth, and they would all be fresh out of available planets to call home.

The Chairwoman adjourned the meeting, attempting to exhibit enthusiasm for *some* of the new directions her staff had discussed. Not a single plan graduated from blind brainstorming to workable theory. In reality, the meeting ended with the same death sentence atmosphere that had capped these gatherings for years. As the board shuffled out of the room, the Scientist knew that his career was effectively over. The decades he had in front of him would be long indeed if his legacy was already tied to the regurgitation of ideas previously reserved for the fantasy of H.G. Wells.

Somehow, he managed to put his things together and leave the conference room. Adding irritation to the insult that had long since overtaken his original injury, the Chairwoman's Chief Aide joined him in the lift down to the Institute's energy lab.

"I'm sorry the meeting went the way it did," the Aide said once the lift doors closed.

"You're not."

The Aide laughed in agreement. "You try to present that idea of yours as a serious alternative; you can't be shocked that this is the response."

"It would work," the Scientist maintained.

"How?" It was the Aide's first sensible question that afternoon, perhaps in his entire life.

"I—" the Scientist began before a sour taste filled his mouth. He only just then realized his critics may have a point. "I don't know yet."

"Sounds like you need a miracle," the Aide said as the lift continued its descent. "Or the October Archive."

# CHAPTER FOUR

MONDAY, OCTOBER 16, 2000
6:02 AM EST
ITERATION 343
MANHATTAN, NEW YORK
EARTH

Sleep did not come quickly, but it did eventually arrive. Orson stayed away from the bedroom and its various creature comforts, as it seemed both too strange to relent to the current conditions of his cage, and that avoiding the bed may have been the only form of protest still available to him. Orson's agitation may not have exclusively been tied to his incarceration. It may have had far more to do with the two hours he spent glued to a television program centered around a political discussion that was 0% thesis, 10% digression and 90% screaming from the participants that served only to remind one another they were still alive. Orson did eventually drift off while splayed out on the living room sofa.

Orson woke fitfully several times in the course of the night, each time in the vague hope that Kan-ur was wrong and his current circumstance was a dream. The couch provided minimal comfort, but the bed still seemed like surrender. Somewhere between the third and seventh instance of waking up with a start he realized a woman was in the apartment with him.

Orson flailed upon the realization he was not alone. The lack of friction between his garment and the almost identically upholstered sofa caused him to slip and hit the floor with a dull thud. He rose to his feet quickly despite a comprehensive ache replacing his body. He tried to focus through the light, but his disorientation got the better of him.

"Who are you?" Orson asked.

"Calm down," the intruder pled with Orson.

"Computer off," Orson attempted the only command he had mastered after his dinner with Kan-ur.

"I'm not the damn digital assistant," the woman insisted. "Lights off," she said as the room filled with darkness. Orson ought to have tried that. He might have slept better if he had.

The woman darted towards the front door. Even with the diminished light, Orson was better able to focus on the woman once she stopped moving.

"The diner," Orson said softly, and then continued more clearly. "You were the woman who ran out of the diner in Woodstock."

She kneeled at the door, pulling out a small glass rectangle from the pack on her back.

"Yes," she said. "You're coming with me. If my luck improves, I'll get you back home before too much damage is done."

Despite Orson's qualms about Kan-ur's ovations to enlist his help, this woman didn't instill much confidence either.

"Why run out of the diner only to try and kidnap me now?"

She grimaced at the word "kidnap". "I got word that they were coming for you. If we didn't get out of there before they arrived, Kan-ur would have vaporized us without a second thought," she said the alien's name with such bile behind her voice. Orson had yet to encounter anyone who didn't treat the mysterious extra-terrestrial with anything worse than terrified reverence.

"Does my savior have a name?"

The intruder's screen blinked on after she placed it against the locked door. It showed an image of the hallway beyond. Four armed guards patrolled at various points leading to the elevator.

"Dammit," she spat.

"I've never met anyone named Dammit before." Despite Orson's uncertainty, he moved closer to the door. "How did you get in here?"

"In is the easy part," she said. "I got in here hours ago while you were engaged in a battle of wits with the bathroom mirror. Getting out will be impossible, now you're the most heavily guarded man in the solar system. You must have really pissed that son of a bitch off. What did you say to him?"

"I—" Orson began, but fell silent as one of the guards moved closer to the door.

"I suppose we could try the air vents," Dammit muttered to herself. "How would you rather die? With them seeing you or hearing you?"

"The core question of my life... Are you saying if someone could get those guards out of the hallway, we can get out of here?"

"Mr. Welles, it's the year 2000. If our path is devoid of armed guards, there's nothing we can't do."

65

\*     \*     \*

First Guard Reilly Goodman normally enjoyed his job. Assigned to the inconsequential sky rise living quarters on the south side of the island, he had a lot of time to think about any number of subjects that had nothing to do with his assigned duties. Mostly his thoughts veered towards vain attempts to remember the lyrics of TV show theme songs from the 80's. He had also begun during those long night shifts to quietly nurse an idea for a novel about a group of modern men searching for the long-lost sword of Arthurian legend, Excalibur. Unfortunately, he was having a hell of a time with how the story should end, and at a complete loss for an opening line.

Now that he guarded someone of such apparent importance, he had to stay alert and focused. Chairman Kan-ur made it clear that dire fates would be in store for anyone who performed their duties less than optimally. The syntax was ominous; the hairs on the back of Goodman's neck had yet to settle.

"You foolish guards..." a voice called out. It sounded as if it came from all directions at once. Goodman aimed his sidearm at all the subsequent places from which he thought the taunt originated. He found the voice familiar, save for some strange quality that made the tone impossible to place. The harsh cackle that followed it ruined any hope he had of finally identifying the call.

"Wha—?" Baker called out. He was Goodman's direct supervisor, and an aggressively worthless person. "Who's there? Where are you?!"

"I'm over here!" the voice called out again. For an instant, it seemed to be coming from the air vents. "Or perhaps I'm over here?" It now seemed to be coming from the elevator door.

Baker opened fire, causing a section of the vent and a panel near the elevator to glow red with his indiscriminate destruction. Goodman wondered in that moment if he should have applied for Baker's job after all.

"I'm already headed for the lobby, you fools!" The voice cackled once more, fading from earshot.

Baker gestured for most of the guards to follow him, but went out of his way to stop Goodman from proceeding. "In case he comes back."

Had he worked anywhere else, Goodman might have feared the grimace he shot at Baker would be taken as insubordination. As it stood, it joined a long list of ignored eye rolls and sighs.

As the elevator door closed behind the guards, Reilly Goodman was once again left alone in his duties, although he sadly got the sinking feeling that he would have to concentrate more closely on his duties than ever before.

\*     \*     \*

Dammit lowered Orson from his perch in front of the apartment's main vent. She then went back to looking at her screen. Much to her confusion and delight, only one guard remained.

"You see? Just like *The Shadow*," Orson beamed.

"Who?" She pulled a pick from her pack and went to work on the door.

"The Shadow," Orson repeated. "Wealthy playboy socialite by day, dark avenger for justice by night..."

She forced the door open and made quick work of the remaining guard, firing a gun that appeared to come from nowhere. The weapon burst forth with a tightly focused projectile that appeared to be the offspring of a flame and a lightning bolt. She just as quickly returned the weapon to her bag. Once the guard fell to the floor, she turned back to Orson.

"You mean like Batman?" she asked.

"What?" Orson's mind was more than a little occupied with the question of whether the guard on the floor was alive or dead.

"Batman. Wealthy playboy socialite by day dark avenger for just—"

"So is this 'Bat man' thing a man or a bat?"

"He's—" Dammit began. "I'm just now realizing it's impossible to explain this concept to someone who's never heard of it."

She checked the guard, indicating to Orson silently that there was at least a small chance that he was still alive. "Come on," Dammit led Orson to the recently returned elevator.

\*     \*     \*

They reached the roof long before the guards began to suspect they had been tricked.

Another flying craft idled on the top of the building. It had little in common with Kan-ur's massive conveyance. The new ship possessed the dimensions of a double decker bus turned on its side. Someone—presumably Orson's new captor—had scrawled the word "Oneida" in scorched black lettering across the ship's hull. While the new machine consisted of the same material as everything else Orson had seen, its configuration was far more erratic. Kan-ur's ship was akin to the finest bed sheets and the *Oneida* to the oldest quilt imaginable. Its haphazard assembly did nothing to alleviate Orson's fears, and he stopped dead among the gravel strewn roof.

"I'm not going in there," Orson insisted.

Dammit's next move occurred with zero hesitation. She whipped around to consider Orson, the gun she used to bring down the lone guard brought to bear. She clicked a control on the weapon. Its machinery emitted a faint whine. In the thick Dr. Pepper-like air around them, small wisps of steam spiraled off the weapon. Dammit only then took a quick glance around to see if the authorities were closing in on their escape, or if her discussion with Orson was worth continuing.

"I'm not going to ask you again, O—Mr. Welles," she said.

Orson's hand went up. "All you had to do was ask." He followed Dammit up the craft's ramp.

\*　　\*　　\*

His rescue now officially a high-stakes prisoner transfer, Orson considered the new craft's interior while Dammit brought the machine to life. It looked less like a vehicle for a real-life Buck Rogers, and more like an impromptu shelter built from pieces found in a junkyard. While he couldn't fathom how one might pilot Kan-ur's machine, he wasn't even sure this new ride *had* any sort of piloting controls.

The ground lurched below him as the ship activated to groaning, unsettling life. The windows went dark as the craft made quick work of exiting the atmosphere. Orson had to brace himself on one of the ship's ramshackle panels. He nearly bumped a large red button in the process.

"Don't touch that," Dammit hissed.

Orson corrected his stance and supported himself with some other nearby fixture. "Don't touch what?"

"The decompression controls," she explained. "That is

unless one of your grossly overrated skills is an ability to breathe in the vacuum of space, then by all means."

"That's a perfectly asinine place to house such a lethal device." Despite his objection, Orson did as he had been told and kept his distance from the crimson control.

"We've had to piece this ship together from what we could find. I'll be sure to pass your objections along to the designer." Dammit rose from her seat and moved to a shelf. Five dark red glass cubes sat upon it. She slapped a corner of each of the objects as they in turn ignited and whirred. Orson moved cautiously to the one seat that appeared to be farthest from any sensitive equipment.

"At least he's trying to save humanity," Orson said. The seat's safety harness automatically tightened after he clicked the buckle together. It made his chest hurt.

Dammit stopped what she was doing. If she meant for the gesture to menace Orson, it was spectacularly efficient. "Who?"

"Kan-ur," Orson explained. "For whatever reason you both think I need to be locked up, Kan-ur's end goal is the continuation of humankind. What's your exc—?"

One by one, the cubes auto-loaded into a tube connected to the shelf. After more mechanized caterwauling within the ships innards, Orson saw the ship spit the cubes out into the cosmos. The precise placement of the objects did not appear to matter in the slightest, as their deployment did not stop Dammit from jumping from her chair, moving directly for Orson and bracing her arm against his windpipe. Orson had seconds before he shifted from a hazy, relaxed reality to outright unconsciousness. It felt as if minutes passed before she released the pressure.

"That's really what he told you, isn't it?" she asked.

Occupied with regaining his breath, Orson did not answer. The ship lurched beneath their feet, and Dammit temporarily lost her balance. Without another word, she returned to her earlier station to regain control over her course.

Orson looked out the craft's window and saw the cubes disappear like the taillights of a car speeding away. When the lights completely disappeared, the ship dipped back in to the glowing grey atmosphere. The floor around him rumbled, gravity altered, and Orson felt the focal point of the turn homestead in his pelvis.

When Orson was able to refocus on his surroundings, the sky filled their view once more. He saw a battalion of ships heading towards them from the far end of the northern hemisphere. He couldn't be completely positive— about anything at this point—but their flashing red and blue lights strongly suggested they were looking for him and other accomplices.

Although conditions might have been better with his previous captor, the likelihood of being blasted out of the sky made the question of Orson's current loyalty a purely pragmatic matter. He quietly thanked whatever might be left of God in this time and place when Dammit banked the ship hard and the view ports showed clear flying straight out into the Atlantic Ocean.

The ship jolted forward. With a lurch they moved no more than several dozen meters before stopping entirely.

"Damn it!" cried Dammit. She slammed her fist on the dashboard.

"What?" Orson asked. He expected any form of an answer would be beyond the scope of his ability to fix. To be fair, that would have been the case with any vehicle more technologically advanced than a sled.

She changed the vessel's heading once more towards the oncoming armada.

"You want to hear *my* excuse for taking you?" Dammit

asked.

"Not anymore."

"You want to know the truth?"

"I believe I already answered that question."

"You want to see the great future of humanity?" She pushed a lever forward to its limit, and the vehicle pushed forward with far more confidence and velocity than before. "Fine by me," she remarked evenly amidst their speed.

Their craft shot through the oncoming horde, using the authorities' confusion as their only defense. Bolts of white-hot plasma sprinkled the sky. On some level, Orson was aware that the bursts of light posed a danger, but they too-closely resembled a fireworks display to instill palpable fear in him.

"Don't you have some type of weaponry on this thing?" Orson asked.

"Ha!" Dammit spat as she pulled the craft upward sharply in response to nearly colliding with one of the police vehicles. "You lack imagination!"

As the red, hazy rising sun filled the portholes, the harsh crackle of a vehicle collision behind them told Orson that Dammit had no need for weapons on the ship. In their zeal, the police would take care of each other.

This back and forth went on for several tense minutes. Dammit was fond of pulling up quickly to befuddle their pursuers, almost as if her default position was to point towards the heavens. Eventually, after only the swiftest police ships remained did she appear to make good on her threat. She pulled up again, but did not immediately bank down to compensate; further and further, they made their way for the sky. She toggled a control near the device Orson guessed was the yoke. A display of the craft's reverse view appeared in front of her. Sure enough, the last two craft maintained their pursuit.

Dammit laughed, re-focusing on the path ahead and beyond.

"What's so funny?" Orson asked.

"It never fails. They will always over-estimate the capacity of their machines, even when they know damn well what their limits are." The clouds around them were growing thicker by the second. In the rear display, Orson could see the two craft backing off.

"The police?"

"Men."

Solid white clouds filled the ship's windows, which then peeled away to reveal the flaked dark of the cosmos. As it turned out, their situation had not improved. A vast armada of ships resembling—but far more massive than—Kan-ur's original vessel floated in front of them.

Orson moaned at the sight of a new batch of obstacles. Slipping past the confines of Earth at their current speed, the two felt the insistently high level of gravity remain once they were past the atmosphere. This feeling did not give way to weightlessness, as Dammit struck another lever and gravity slowly returned to normal.

Several of the larger ships made their approach as Dammit pulled the ship around once more, gunned the engines, and started their most daring drop of the flight yet. The windows filled with fire as they re-entered the atmosphere. This was only a brief flash of red light before the scene resumed its normal color once more. The two crafts that had so doggedly pursued them were now in a steep descent. Smoke billowed from their engines as they fell.

Dammit attempted pulling out of their fall. The ship refused to respond until just before they would have exploded across Sixth Avenue. A vaguely amused expression settled on Dammit's face as she weaved between buildings without any further interference; Orson took the opportunity to settle into a long period of nausea from which he did not expect to emerge. Once they were clear of the city, Dammit pivoted the craft east, to the dark, vaguely foreboding country beyond the relative tranquility of Manhattan.

\*     \*     \*

Orson normally viewed any trip into the wild wasteland of New Jersey as a march into the bowels of Hell. As the *Oneida* crossed the radioactive sewage that was once the Hudson River, Orson's previous histrionics became undeniable reality.

The earth was scorched past the seeming refuge of humanity that was the eastern seaboard. Life could not survive—to say nothing of thrive—in an environment such as this. Trees seemed like a distant memory, and dark patches of vegetation mocked the idea that grass might have once existed. Dammit brought the ship in for a landing on a large outcropping of dry salt-like Earth. The sky around them burned with a dark crimson hue, almost like pooled blood. The ship's display marked the local time as just past nine in the morning, but the sun remained truant. Dammit flicked another switch and the space in front of them flooded with light and horror.

Thin, weak ghouls of what might have once been people flooded the area. From the air, Orson figured the creatures for cockroaches, but only now realized that notion to be foolish. Naked and without any sign of what Orson would have considered civilization, they roamed desperately in front of the ship, slow to realize that Orson and Dammit's presence was anything outside of their normal experience.

"Welcome to Princeton." Dammit cut the power to the ship's engines.

"I was never much for college," Orson whispered, for fear that the creatures beyond might hear him.

"This is Kan-ur's bright future for humanity. Scattered cities of relative comfort for few, and a whole planet worth of rejects beyond." Dammit infused her voice with no inflection. Orson could tell her terror was nevertheless present, merely encased in a numb cocoon.

"It's like something out of an H.G. Welles novel." Orson's voice had no volume. "How did they beco—?"

"—are you going to give me any more trouble?" Dammit asked. She took great pains to not look at Orson and keep her eyes on the horror in front of her.

Orson decided as early as their departure from Manhattan not to resist his new captor's instructions any further. He wasn't ready to say he trusted her—or anyone, for that matter—but was still content with his conclusion. He nodded.

"Ready to leave?" she asked.

Out in the lit distance, Orson could see a group of the creatures—he hesitated to use the word "people", but even that hesitance filled him with a dull, nebulous guilt—hunched over something. When they looked up at the ship's lights, Orson then realized they had been feeding on one of their own.

"Yes. I'm ready to leave."

The larger mass of the population made its way towards them. Dammit restarted the engines far too slowly for Orson's tastes. Their slow, lumbering approach only made the sudden pounding on the walls surrounding Orson and Dammit all the more startling.

With glassy eyes, Dammit kicked the machine into gear. A wave of nausea crashed over Orson as the dull pounding continued with the craft's ascension.

Dammit pulled a thin metallic disc from her control board connected by a coiled wire. She brought the object to her mouth. "October survives," she said weakly into the device. Her words boomed forth in all directions, amplified by the ship's machinery. She replaced the disc and increased the craft's acceleration. It was at least half a minute and well into the thickening of the sickly purple cloud cover before whatever was trying to get into the ship stopped banging on the wall and drifted away.

"Was that supposed to comfort them, that little speech of yours?" Orson asked.

"Me more than them."

The purple gave way to the darkness of space beyond, and it was only after realizing the fleet hovering above Manhattan was hundreds if not thousands of miles away that Orson chose to speak again.

"Who is October?" Orson asked.

Dammit moved farther away from the Earth, so that the only thing Orson could see was a field of stars. One of them, Orson noticed, was red. She locked the craft into place, and the yoke she had so expertly steered moved back into the dashboard with a mechanical whir. Another panel flipped down revealing a large red button. All the while, Dammit said nothing.

"You can ask him yourself," Dammit finally answered, then pushed the button.

\*    \*    \*

MONDAY, OCTOBER 16TH, 2000
4:07 PM COORDINATED MARTIAN TIME
ITERATION 343
APPROACHING PHOBOS, THE SECOND MOON

## MARS

The planet Mars was not at all what Orson Welles had expected. Upon closer inspection, the planet's eerie canals—visible even to men of his time—did not hide an indigenous Martian population. Instead, large industrial cables emanated from the crevasses, spitting sparks of power. Bisecting one half of the crimson orb was a large metal arc that made the planet resemble Saturn with an identity crisis.

Dammit said nothing to him for the nearly 230 million miles between the planets, except for one lone statement when the image of Mars in the porthole was just ever so slightly larger than Orson's thumb.

"I apologize for being so short with you earlier," she said to him. "The name is Rebecca." She had not taken her eyes away from the growing red dot, so much so that Orson spent the next twenty minutes of the voyage wondering if Rebecca had offered her apology to him, or Mars itself.

Orson maintained his silence until the strange arc was more fully in view and could no longer be confused for anything other than the mysterious object it appeared to be.

"What's that?" Orson asked.

"The largest McDonalds franchise in the solar system," Rebecca only then realized her mistake. "There aren't going to be any references that won't fly over your head, are there?"

"What's there to understand?" Orson asked through his befuddlement. "In the future, there's some mad Scottish robber baron erecting metallic arches all over the planet."

Rebecca smiled despite herself. For the first time in the journey, Orson felt like he might not die on this journey.

"You're quicker than I thought you'd be." She said nothing for the rest of the trip.

*　　*　　*

The *Oneida* landed in an area that highlighted Orson's diminishing quality of life. In stark contrast to the shimmering Manhattan platform that inaugurated his incarceration, the Phobos Base hangar door jerked open with a lurch to let them in, and sealed them within its confines with an even more labored action.

Rebecca shut down the vessel and turned her pilot's seat around. She pulled a lever and Orson's constraints retreated back from where they came. For a moment, she didn't get up and just eyed Orson wearily.

He put his hands up. "No trouble."

Rebecca gestured for Orson to follow her as she walked down the gangway.

The hangar was in even worse shape up close than it appeared from above. The floors were dirty with boulders of Martian rock and a heavy amount of dust. The condition of the facility went beyond the rustic quality of a place well-lived in and firmly into the territory of neglect. The wafting, spoiled sulfur smell didn't help matters.

Rebecca continued to lead Orson further into the facility. The corridor they travelled through was a slight improvement over the hangar, although the sulfur remained, and the flickering yellow light threatened to deepen Orson's headache. Halfway down the passage, they came upon a large stone object. It was ancient and crumbling and depicted what appeared to be a stern man with aquiline features obscured only by a long beard and a thick mane of hair.

"Is that October?" Orson asked as he stopped to

consider the object.

Rebecca laughed, only allowing for the interruption of their movement for a brief moment. "Hardly."

"Is it a Martian?"

"No. Don't be simple." She looked at the statue once more. "At least, I don't think so. Whatever it was, it's ancient history now. Come on."

After the corridor, they were in another large cavernous room. The teeming mass of people populating the chamber lay somewhere between the angelic fools of Manhattan and the horrible wretches Orson witnessed in the rest of the country. They appeared sturdy, rugged, and able to handle themselves in a fight. The last time Orson even imagined this many people with eye patches and missing limbs, they occurred to him via the works of Robert Louis Stevenson. Upon their entrance, every last occupant of the large room stared directly at Orson. All other activities ceased, except for Rebecca's steady march towards a final set of dirty white doors.

When Orson finally caught up to her, Rebecca gestured for him to go on without her. "This is where I leave you."

"But we've had such a grand time," Orson retorted.

Rebecca said nothing and appeared to fight the growth of a smirk on her face. Orson marked the slight struggle as a victory. Not wanting to push his luck with the woman who had pulled a gun on him, then strangled him, all before showing him the deepest bowels of Hell, Orson stepped towards the door. Rebecca put her hand out to stop him.

"What?" Orson asked.

Rebecca looked at the door, then back to Orson. "He's—" she snapped her head. "No. I'm not going to be the one to tell you. I wouldn't dream of ruining the surprise."

"What? How the Hell am I supposed to go in there with something like that hanging over my head?"

Rebecca put her hand up. "Let's just say he's difficult. Good luck."

Orson's brow arced into the shape of a question mark rotated ninety-degrees. Knowing that answers to any questions he had would not be forthcoming from Rebecca, he went through the doors.

Beyond the door was a nearly pitch-black space. A single machine emanating a column of light interrupted the darkness, highlighting a lone figure in the distance. It's resemblance to his first meeting with Kan-ur was the first thing that annoyed Orson. His irritation would not stop there.

"Hello?" Orson called out. "Excuse me, are you Mr. October?"

"George Orson Welles," the figure croaked weakly. "Born May 6th, 1915 to Richard H—"

That was the second thing.

"If you don't mind, sir, I recently heard my *curriculum vitae* from the other fellow. I now suspect you will lie to me. So, let's skip ahead to what you want from me."

The figure labored through a wheezing laugh. "Right you are." He coughed several times in hopes of restoring his lungs to a normal rhythm. "You have always viewed yourself as the heir to Shakespeare. You too will move the world by way of the stage. I may be presumptuous, but I'd be willing to guess you feel like your career has stalled before it even began."

Orson added one more irritation to his list of grievances. "I heard all of this from the other fellow as well," Orson lied. Kan-ur's praise had been so effusive, Orson had intermittently forgotten he was a prisoner.

"Yes," the figure said in a tone that, in its strength, was

completely at odds with the tentative way the figure stumbled towards Orson. "But what the Great Kan-ur didn't tell you, Mr. Welles, is that your supposed destiny is complete tripe. You're a terror to everyone you meet. You're far more trouble than you're worth. In fact, Mr. Welles, you are quite simply too dangerous to be allowed to walk free."

Orson felt the distinct sensation of quiet, futile desperation that could only be recreated when being scolded by his father. He spent such sparse time with the elder Welles before his death fifteen—or seventy, depending on your perspective—years earlier, but the feeling was unmistakable.

"And what brings you to that conclusion, sir?" Orson managed to ask when he was able to ignore the hot, flushed feeling in his face.

The figure stepped into the light. He was elderly and rail-thin like his followers. He was slightly shorter than Orson, although his reliance on his cane may have obscured the man's true stature. He wore the same plain black tunic and slacks that Orson had pilfered from the Manhattan apartment. His eyes were wide, ultimately making his expression less inquisitive and more annoyed. The old man had little hair, and what remained shined white in the machine's glow. He pursed his mouth forward, as if he was trying and failing to understand the younger man.

"Young man, I'm the one they call October. I know what evil lurks in the hearts of men, to say nothing of your own."

The man's face and the voice came together in recognition for Orson in that moment. He had heard too much of that voice for his own good, and had seen the face—or some version of it—each time he looked in the mirror.

The man standing in front of Orson Welles was none other than Orson Welles.

# CHAPTER FIVE

"You're—" Orson's next words stymied him.

"Go on—" the man who identified himself as October encouraged him.

"—ancient!"

"Bah! I'm eighty-five years old, and we were born the same year! Let's just hope when you get to my age, you'll look half as good as this."

"You're—" Orson began.

"Go on..." October tried again. "I'd say I've heard it all before, but I suppose it would be more accurate to say I've said it all before."

"You're *me*," Orson finally said.

October took a harsh step forward and regarded his younger self with contempt.

"Let us get one thing absolutely certain between us." October whispered the words, although his low volume may have had something to do with the wheezing whistle of his breath. "You are *not* me. You are under no circumstances to equate yourself with me. If you stray from this rule, you will reckon with my wrath."

October stared Orson down for a long moment.

Eventually convinced he made his point, the old man turned back to the glowing workstation in front of them.

"Now hold on!" Orson croaked as he followed his older self. "Between me, myself, I, the broad with the pilot's license, and the asshole with a fish bowl for a head, I would hope that, of all people I would at the very least be able to trust mys—"

The words evaporated suddenly as Orson fell to the floor with a slam. October now stood over him, holding his cane like a sword. Putting the last second or two together in his head, Orson realized the old man had hooked him just under the knee with his walking aid and knocked him off his feet. October was now holding the edge of the cane only an inch or so from Orson's face. The old man appeared to maintain balance with or without his stick. Orson could never before have imagined feeling such a mixture of a headache, terror, and relief while contemplating what growing old would actually mean for him.

"You," October regarded Orson as if he were speaking to a child. "Are *not* me."

Orson nodded quickly, his hands raised in supplication. October returned his attention back to the workstation and hit one of the machine's countless buttons. Appearing before them, as if it too had made the trip from the Earth to Mars, was the creature that had previously identified itself by the name of "Schmoogle Boogle."

"Hi there!" the wraith croaked after he was brought to life. "I'm Schmoogle Boogle, your friendly digital assistant engine! Can I interest you in some po—?"

"Please inform Rebecca that she can come in now," October ordered.

"You got it!" S.B. squeaked, but he didn't immediately disappear. "You might also be interested in this list," S.B.

conjured a single photograph out of thin air depicting a woman with a shocked look on her face. "Of five cats that look exactly like Chairman Ka—"

"Just do it," October bellowed. Without further inquiry, S.B. disappeared to its work.

Rebecca entered the room almost instantly after S.B.'s departure. She did not seem fazed by Orson's position on the floor, or by the fact that two Orsons currently occupied the room.

"Is everything ready?" October asked while neglecting to look at Rebecca.

"Yes sir." A nervous undercurrent permeated her voice. Such uncertainty would have been completely implausible to Orson previously. "All the transmitting amplifiers have been planted per your instructions."

October said nothing more to her for a moment. "Keep an eye on *him*, will you?" he finally barked. "We're about to go live."

Rebecca helped Orson to his feet. Orson's indignant expression was likely not the appropriate response to his unique situation. He didn't care.

"What?" Rebecca kept her voice down.

"How the hell do I know if you are the virtuous ones, eh?" Orson was also careful not to speak above a whisper or take his eyes away from the busy October. "I saw those ghastly things you showed me, but how do I know *you* didn't put them there?"

"I have three things to say to you, Mr. Welles," October said from a distance. "First, you can't know that we *are* the proverbial good guys based on the information available, so don't try.

"Second, the only reason you're willing to accept Kanur's version of events is because he chose not to see through your finely cultivated air of bullshit and instead lavish you with the undue praise that had fueled your entire life.

"Third, if you don't cease your prattling, Rebecca there will shoot you without a second thought. She's a modern girl and is not possessed of the same sentimental attachment to human life that you think you possess. You may have your suspicions about us, young man, but you will be well advised to trust me on that last bit of information."

October fiddled with another control in front of him. "And a fourth thing: I'm eighty-five years old. I'm far closer to the grave than you're even remotely prepared to fathom, but my hearing is just as good, if not better than yours."

The old man manipulated one final lever on the panel and the entire room suddenly filled with light. The room was almost entirely white, as if the sudden illumination was coming from every surface—wall, floor and ceiling. The door through which Rebecca and Orson entered the area, another large door on the wall perpendicular to the entrance, several rows of black chairs, and a final dark streak high on the wall directly across from them provided respite from the blinding change in the room's lighting. Orson swore he could make out the image of cameras just beyond the high dark panel.

S.B. reappeared, looking as if he had no memory of the previous discussion he had with October.

"Hi there! I'm Schmoo—"

"Tell them they can come in now!" October barked.

"Sure thing! In the meantime, you might be interested i—"

"Tell them," October, Rebecca, and Orson snapped in unison. S.B. shut his eyes and the corner door swung open.

October and Rebecca eyed Orson oddly. "What? That

thing can't try my last nerve, too?" Orson asked.

People filed in and took those seats Orson and Rebecca did not already occupy. Some of them Orson had seen on his way into his audience with October. In further contrast to those people Orson saw back on Earth, they were neither the angelic nitwit civilians consumed with their tunnel vision, nor the militaristic automatons that spent their days in service to Kan-ur. The earnestness of these people only served to deepen Orson's doubt, especially when they wouldn't stop staring at him as if he were the oddest thing in the room. His frustration with their gawking ebbed only when he realized that, given their leader, he might just be the strangest man they've seen in some time.

Rebecca monitored the orderly arrival and seating of the incoming people, all the while keeping an eye on Orson. When everyone was in their assigned places, Rebecca returned to October's side.

"Everything is ready," she told the old man.

October looked up from his work and nodded. He then grabbed Rebecca's hand, which sent Orson's confusion soaring towards the asteroid belt. It was only after Orson realized that October handed her a small device that she immediately placed in her ear that Orson's befuddlement came back down to Earth. Or Mars. Whichever planet was closer.

Four dim red lights flashed across the black wall panel. The room then went dark once again. A single bright spot from above brought October into sharp relief.

"I offer greetings to all of humanity. My name is Orson Welles..." October trailed off. Orson flinched not only at October's clear effort to avoid looking in Orson's direction, not only at the uneven timbre in his older self's performance, but primarily because with the massive audience now watching, Orson couldn't help but envy himself.

"At least, that was my name a long time ago. You have come to know me these last sixty years as October, the human voice of Kan-ur's wishes. Fifteen years ago, I appeared on Merv Griffin and proclaimed that I would no longer be a party to the lies of our supposed savior from the stars, nor would I tacitly endorse the bloodshed he wills to be a part of our lives."

"What the hell is a Merv Griffin?" Orson asked Rebecca *sotto voce*. She shushed him.

"In response to my insolence, Kan-ur wiped Los Angeles not only from the map, but from our mechanized memory as well. Los Angeles is not placed into our children's minds during their education, and our personal memories have largely been lost to the unending noise of our electrified life. Kan-ur need not even offer you a lie about sudden disaster befalling the Western Coast. You assumed that if a city was there one day and gone the next, that there must have been a valid reason for the change. The price you charge for your complicit cooperation is the comfortable sedation that has become Kan-ur's sole source of currency.

"Many of you wonder why—if Kan-ur delivered us from our own destruction—why would anyone with even an ounce of human feeling dare oppose him? I'm sure those of you that think of this..." In front of October, an image of Kan-ur shimmered into a translucent view similar to S.B. "...*creature* as God, could only logically view me as the devil. If Kan-ur advocates for our continuing survival, then those that oppose him thirst for humanity's annihilation.

"I implore you to believe me when I say that I seek only the greater good. I aim to provide a world free not only of Kan-ur, but of Orson Welles as well. I implore you to break free of the shackles of our benign comfort and resist! Kan-ur plans to re-take our past once more. His plans will prove futile without your cooperation. If we resist, we will take the first steps in determining our own destiny, and we may just save the entire human race—"

The room shuddered around them and the spotlight covering October dimmed. A large chunk of the roof slammed to the ground. The equipment transmitting October's call to arms groaned to inactivity.

"God Damnit! What Happened?" October chose not to move from his current position, but he practically vibrated with frustration.

Rebecca leapt out of her seat and moved her hand to her ear. "They cut the signal. They're here." Another shudder rocked the base. Within seconds, the rest of October's people who assembled in the studio rose to action.

"We were so close," October told Rebecca as they both approached Orson. The younger Welles had also risen from his seat, but only tentatively so. "Let's just hope the larger part of the broadcast made it to Earth before that bastard cut us off."

"I hope it didn't!" Orson shouted over the wail of the facility's emergency sirens.

"Why is that?" Rebecca's confusion bypassed her inclination to accept Orson's remark with hostility. Nothing could diminish October's animosity for Orson.

"You're trading on my face and name!" Orson exasperated. "The least you could do is bring some theatricality to the proceedings. But no, you're content to simply drone on and on like some dehydrated vicar! You call that a speech? If it turns out I have two lives to live, I'd still be thrilled to not waste one of them on whatever those words were supposed to be!"

"We should have killed you when we had the chance!" October growled, and then addressed the larger group. He was careful to avoid eye contact with Orson as he did so. "You all know what this means. Let's go."

"I'm ready," Rebecca told the old man. The three moved towards the main studio door, despite Orson's petulance slowing their progress.

"Were you going to kill me during that broadcast?" Orson asked after Rebecca tried to grab his arm as if he were nothing more than an errant child.

"It was disc—" Rebecca began to confess.

"It's the last time I let the powers that be change one of my endings, I assure you," October said.

"That's not the issue!" Orson cried.

"Settle down," October ordered. "I won't kill you. The moment passed. If you live through the next few hours, you might be of some use to humanity yet. Now, get into the ship before I change my mind," he concluded as they re-entered the shoddy hangar containing the *Oneida*.

"I—" Orson attempted to protest, but then opted for a move towards the ship. "I really do hate you," he did manage to add as he walked up the gangway.

"I am absolutely fine with that," October replied as he followed.

\*    \*    \*

The hangar opened and spit the *Oneida* into a battle nearing its end. The fleet that had nearly ended Orson's flight from Earth was in full force across the Martian skies. A fleet of ships from October's ramshackle forces met another group of ships loyal to Kan-ur in the air surrounding the arch. To see it out of the porthole window in front of Orson, he imagined wooden dinghies attempting to overtake an Ironclad, if the dinghies came complete with weapons discharging bright flashes of light.

"If they got here this fast, there's no way we'll ever know if the message left orbit," Rebecca observed. She kept the *Oneida* out of the fray of the battle, but their safety would not last long.

"It'll be the last mistake I'll ever make," October croaked, which flowed nearly seamlessly into Orson clearing his throat in response. "Then again, I've been wrong before."

"Which one is Kan-ur's flagship?" Rebecca asked.

"Bah!" October spat. "He'll be on the ship furthest from the action. Mark my words; he'll let the others die for him."

"What makes you s—?"

A ship in the distance—it was impossible to tell if it was allied with October or Kan-ur—exploded, distracting Orson both from concluding his remark and from the moment October used his metal cane to strike Orson over the head.

"Stop talking," October ordered.

"You're a bit self-destructive, you know that?" Orson's head buzzed from the impact, but the pain felt as if it existed just outside his head. He opted not to rub the site of the injury, as he instead occupied his hands with remaining steady in his seat.

"I had it coming," October said.

Throughout their exchange, Rebecca piloted the vessel through the battle and beyond, to a large ship in orbit around Deimos, the only of Mars's two moons currently visible.

"I think I've found it," Rebecca told them after their *tête-à-tête* descended into October holding his cane in an attack stance, and Orson rubbing his throbbing head. The two men—if temporarily—forgot their disagreements to focus on what she had found.

The likeliest candidate for Kan-ur's flagship remained unmoved by their advance.

"That's him," October said firmly.

"The ship could have been deployed later than the others," Rebecca theorized.

"Just like us," Orson offered.

"Careful," October warned.

"Wasn't that the point of your little speech down there? You're exactly the same as him, except you were visited in the night by the Ghost of Genocides Past?"

October stared at Orson. "Rebecca, hold your breath my dear. My desire to kill him is coming back, and I think I might decompress the cabin—"

"Silence, the both of you!" Rebecca said. She might have also included the ship in the order, as every indicator light on her dashboard came to inscrutable life. Orson had previously been unable to comprehend the controls of the craft, but now with its cacophony of bright information, even he could tell some condition had changed. "That ship is headed straight for the arch."

"They've had it on since they brought our young friend back. They can't have more than a few hours to send everyone back before Mars' core won't have enough energy for another trip," October said.

"What could he be planning?" Rebecca asked while taking the initiative to engage in a pursuit course.

"Don't you see? He isn't planning at all," said October. "He's scrambling and sloppy and that can only mean we're winning. Follow that ship!"

Rebecca did nothing different just then, but still appeared to all present as if she were dutifully following

October's orders. Their ship was faster than any of the large sentry vessels currently employed by Kan-ur, and as such they were able to catch up to their suspect long before it was within striking distance of the now-glowing arch.

Rebecca pulled their ship alongside its larger counterpart, and there they stayed for several long, cross-fire filled seconds.

"What are you doing?" October wheezed. "Board them for Christ's sake."

"I'm—" Rebecca struggled with both her words and the managing of their flight path. "I'm trying. I think they are trying to capture us at the same time."

"Well, stop them!" Orson cried. He hadn't felt this useless in a conversation since his wedding.

"They're trying to take us on board, we're trying to get on board," Rebecca hissed, still struggling with the ship. "Why don't we just acknowledge that—for the moment—our goals are the same and just lean into it, hmm?"

Both men put their hands up in deference to the decision now out of either of their hands. Rebecca re-directed her attention to the controls and locked them into place.

\*   \*   \*

Despite the escalation of the battle outside, the hangar deck of Kan-ur's ship was a haven of relative peace and calm. The serenity ceased when a small pod appeared to be on a collision course. Most of the technicians and launch personnel on deck instantly recognized the intruder as an emergency release from one of the ancient X1029 corvettes currently engaging them in battle. Those personnel were far more surprised as it flew through the outer gate and crashed with a chaotic rush of air at the far end of the chamber.

The technicians moved to render assistance, never once giving any serious thought to the reality that enemy combatants were likely in the pod. They didn't have time to consider that unfortunate reality as a contingent of guards quickly marched into the hangar and took positon around the smoking wreck.

"What the hell happened in here?" the Sergeant spat as he took in the crash zone.

"What the hell are you morons doing here?" the Foreman spat back. She had long since learned that if one neglected to show fear, the average guard wouldn't know what to do with himself.

The Sergeant and the Foreman were interrupted as one of the battle-scarred corvettes from the battle beyond followed a similar path as its vanguard. It knocked several of the moored attack ships off their landing skids before coming to a screeching halt in the middle of the hangar.

Now possessed of larger problems than the stray escape pod, the troopers and mechanics swarmed towards the second crashed ship to either render assistance, or eliminate all survivors. So focused were they on this latest development, that not one of them noticed the explosive decompression of the escape pod's hatch and three survivors sneaking out of the smaller ship.

Despite looking shaken by the flight, the old man led the way out of the hangar. Rebecca lagged behind to eye her fallen ship. When he realized that Orson was now the only one following him, he whipped around on his cane and grabbed Rebecca's arm.

"I really liked that ship," Rebecca lamented.

October shot a worried glance at the ship's workers, knowing their distraction would not be indefinite. "We'll get you another one! Come on!" he hissed, putting no volume behind the plea.

*    *    *

"There's a what?" Kan-ur asked sharply.

"A fire, sir!" the ship's S.B. unit replied. This projection of the ubiquitous program appeared sharper, or perhaps more severe than his civilian counterparts. This quality had less to do with the whimsical predilections of the Schmoogle Boogle Corporation and their design team, but more with the basic intelligence at the program's core. The program behaved more seriously with the knowledge of the weaponry at its disposal.

"On this ship?" Kan-ur asked.

"In the hangar, yes sir!" S.B. responded.

The assembled crew on the command deck had become accustomed to the various rages and moods of the chairman, even if they did not have a face to read. Only October in his prime could have rivaled them in their intimate knowledge of Kan-ur. Some of them supposed October might still know Kan-ur better than anyone, if the rumors about his survival were true. The current situation—with conflicting reports of multiple anarchist ships crashing into the stern of this vessel—was far too strange for any actual human to read the mood of the dark figure that led them.

The doors to the control door slid open, revealing Rebecca, Orson, and October.

Kan-ur sighed when he saw the three intruders. To Orson, the frustration sounded more like air trapped in a water dispenser. It sounded like that to everyone else assembled as well, but they were far more accustomed to the strange machinations of Kan-ur's biological processes.

"That will be all, computer," Kan-ur finally said when

the noise had run its course. S.B. disappeared. "I suppose this fire business was your handiwork?" Kan-ur asked the intruders.

"Sorry to disappoint you, my friend," October replied, indicating Rebecca. "But it was all her."

"I was talking *to* her," Kan-ur clarified. "You never quite had the courage for such a maneuver."

Kan-ur might have continued his taunting of October, or October might have reciprocated further, but the control deck filled suddenly with red light. It was as if the room started to catch fire itself—which was a distinct possibility, given the current condition of the ship.

Everything froze around them. While they maintained awareness of seconds passing, each soul on that deck could feel that they too were no longer governed by the petty constrictions of time. If S.B. were active at that moment, it would have experienced a number of errors related to its internal clock.

Then, in an instant that felt like it transpired over the course of an hour, time seemed to skip backward several seconds.

"Either of you," Kan-ur finally said to both Orsons Welles after the red light cleared away.

"What the hell was that?" Orson asked. As he spoke, his lips were no longer in sync with his words. Kan-ur could only guess as to whether he asked the question before his last statement.

"Oh, Mr. Welles," Kan-ur mocked injury. His cynicism now undeniable, Orson realized he was now witness to the true Kan-ur. The gesture may have cemented for all time where Orson's loyalty would truly lie.

"I thought you would be relieved," Kan-ur continued. He nodded to one of the technicians on the control deck. They in turn manipulated some controls, and activated the main viewer.

The image showed Earth, but without the dim coloring or the flying saucers in orbit. Orson looked to Rebecca and October, and both appeared stricken by the sight.

"Your new friends can tell you quite plainly, although I imagine even you can ascertain the truth after everything you've learned on this holiday of yours," Kan-ur explained to Orson as he gleefully took in the agony of the woman and the old man.

After the young man said nothing, Kan-ur felt obligated to accept he may have overestimated one of the Orsons present. "You see, my boy," Kan-ur began, finally spelling out the truth. "October's quest to stop me has failed. On the bright side, you're home."

# CHAPTER SIX

SUNDAY, OCTOBER 30, 1938
9:18 PM COORDINATED MARTIAN TIME
ITERATION 344
JUST BEYOND MARTIAN ORBIT

For the first time in fifteen years—for the first time ever, in truth—the man called October and the thing called Kan-ur agreed completely. As the beautiful, pristine—if only so from a distance—Earth hovered in front of them, the situation was completely hopeless.

"You may be right," October admitted as he approached his nemesis, leaving Rebecca and Orson behind. The rest of Kan-ur's people quickly evacuated the deck without any further order from their leader. They may have not wished to become collateral damage in Kan-ur and October's struggle. The fire alarms blaring also contributed to their urgency. As they left, each member of Kan-ur's coterie eyed October and Orson with an expression that scaled the very limits of incredulity. Moments before, they accepted as gospel that October died ages ago. Now, they could not deny the presence of two

Octobers in one place.

"But there's at least some impact we can make, yet," October concluded.

"How do you figure?"

"First, I managed to break free of your influence. That happened the day I went on with Merv Griffin. That alone will make the next iteration markedly different from any other you've attempted."

"Truly, what in Alighieri's Hell is a Merv Griffin?" Orson asked Rebecca. He did not receive a response as October and Kan-ur moved slowly closer to one another.

"Second, no matter what happens, you're going to have a very hard time convincing my young replacement over there that yours is a just and worthy cause.

"Third, that message—"

Kan-ur wagged his long fingers so close to October's face, Orson half-expected the old man to bite his digits clean off.

"'We blocked your precious transmission rather effectively.'" Surprisingly, October revealed the information. "That's what you're about to say, Kan-ur, isn't it? Save your objections, I know you too well. But, my dear friend, you and I both know that in this technological age you have constructed, the moment a camera is exposed, the recording never truly goes away. You'll be outrunning the specter of that broadcast for the next twenty iterations of your unholy empire.

"Fourth—"

"Fourth?" Kan-ur asked incredulously. "Old man, you must be slipping if you can't make your case using only three points. Where's your sense of structure?"

Despite Kan-ur's attempts to taunt October, Orson got the sense that his older self was finally getting the better of the alien chairman.

"Despite the single rationale for the perverted existence you maintain as a life, you can't keep doing this over and over again!" October continued undeterred.

Kan-ur took a step backward, October's vital blow apparently effective. October cackled at the crumbling of Kan-ur's facade.

"Don't give me that look, Kan-ur," October chastised him.

Orson noted the increasing number of alarms around them, communicating the progress of the fire below them. He became concerned that he would have the unusual experience of burning to death, and then immediately freezing in the empty expanse between Earth and Mars.

"When I was a young man, you brought me to the far-flung future of the year 2015, and now you are trying it all again 15 years earlier. The time between those two points is getting shorter with each—" October lost himself in the middle of a memory. "What did I always call these things?"

"Rehearsals," Orson chimed in.

October snapped his fingers, in that moment deciding that if for nothing other than his clearer memory, his younger self may be of some use. "Yes, indeed! It's getting shorter and shorter with every *rehearsal*. It will do so until one of these trips through the arch will only buy you a week and a half of continued life. When that day comes, I'll be long gone, but some version of me will be there. You, on the other hand, will die, and we'll all be better off without you."

Kan-ur slammed his fist against the control room railing. The action sounded like a rubber hose falling against a concrete floor. He then screamed in a rage and sprang for October. October grabbed for the same railing, swinging his cane around so that the point hovered inches from the tissue connecting Kan-ur's head to his torso.

October squeezed the handle of the cane and a gleaming metal blade extended from the tip.

"You know what this is, don't you?" October twitched the blade slightly as he posed the question to Kan-ur.

The same bubbling sound that Orson equated with Kan-ur's only human quality filled the control room, as the creature twirled away from the point of October's weapon. His head whirred as two gleaming metal blades protruded from the equator of Kan-ur's skull. Kan-ur reached for the metal and removed two brass knuckles with serrated edges, holding them in an attack stance.

Orson noticed that Rebecca moved away from him, and now hovered over one of the deck's many control mechanisms.

Orson approached her, if for no other reason than his certainty that he wanted no part of Kan-ur and October's ongoing exchange. "What are you doing?"

"I'm aiming the weapons at the ships that have already followed us through the arch. Not a lot that bastard can do without anybody following him," she explained. She was intent enough on the work at hand that she barely left a ghost to communicate with Orson. She must have learned the trait from October.

"But you said—" Orson attempted before the sound of Kan-ur and October's struggle made further discussion impossible.

"I also know that no matter what sword you may wield, you are an old man now and unfortunately will grow no younger," Kan-ur said calmly as their weapons clashed.

October smiled as energy bolts exploded just outside the image on the viewer. He leaned against the railing, and Kan-ur continued to advance upon him, as if the Chairman were content merely to toy with the old man. The lights in the control room blinked out and returned in a flash. All four souls could not ascertain whether the unreliability of the electricity resulted from the hangar fire or the now-ambiguous role of this ship in the ongoing battle. They only knew they could not remain stationary for long.

"I'm not as old as you, Kan-ur. No one ever could be."

Kan-ur lashed out; his limbs flailed forward towards October, slicing at his torso. October fell to the ground. With his fleeing strength, he threw his cane across the control room. It landed a few feet away from Orson. Only then did October's younger counterpart realize blood covered the makeshift weapon.

"Rebecca!" October cried out. "There'll be another one! Get rid of it!"

Orson flinched, half-expecting a swift killing blow from behind. Instead, when he turned back to Rebecca her focus remained intent on the weapons console.

"You heard him!" she finally said. "Dump the cane!"

Orson grabbed the weapon, but froze in his ignorance as to what came next. After a few brief moments holding the object, the hair on the back of his neck snapped to attention, and the glow of the weapon answered all of his questions one by one. The only answer still missing at that point was why this relic from his future suddenly lifted his confusion.

"Throw it in the God-damned garbage!" Rebecca repeated as one of their ships made an attack run and the power flickered once more.

Kan-ur opted for an orderly escape over a murder hat trick and fled under the cover of the intermittent darkness.

Orson snapped out of whatever hold the cane had on him and made quick work of finding a dark panel labeled "REFUSE INGRESS." Still trying to contemplate the experience of holding the object, Orson chucked the cane through the panel. The lights around them shut off once more and did not return. Emergency track lighting took over and only served to disorient Orson more. Rebecca pulled herself away from the weapons control and approached Orson.

"Now what do I do?" Orson asked Rebecca as he stared at the trash chute.

"Where this ship is going, it won't matter for much longer." She grabbed his arm.

They moved to October, who still lay supine on the deck where Kan-ur had left him. The amount of blood they had to walk through to reach the old man sealed his—and by extension, Orson's own—fate. October could only manage a cough by way of greeting once he saw Rebecca. She tried vainly to put pressure on his wounds, but the old man pushed her away and instead grabbed her arm.

"You know—" he managed. Rebecca nodded. October then reached out to Orson frantically. Orson tried to keep his distance from his own final moments, but couldn't ignore the old man's gesticulating.

"I—" October began, or more aptly, ended. "I should have—" he rasped, and then fell back.

Orson sat back. The realization that he was sitting in a pool of his own blood was only among the top five most troubling truths confronting him in that moment.

"I may need a moment," Orson finally said. He hoped for more from his own eulogy, but he also never thought he'd be the one giving it.

"That's great," Rebecca said as she grabbed his arm again. Her own mourning for the old man never came, had already passed, or she shoved it back into some deep recess of her mind. "Come on!"

She dragged him to another control panel and entered commands. The ship lurched around underneath them, or at least felt as if it did after Orson felt briefly heavier and the distorted star field around them shifted. The foremost window filled with the far-off sight of another of Kan-ur's ships. A torrent of energy bolts obscured the other ship. The room sank further into darkness for a moment, only to re-light the chamber via a small fire that erupted where one of the other control units had previously stood.

"There!" She went back to her previous position at the weapons console as she locked a lever into place and sprinted for the exit, never relaxing her grip on Orson in the process.

The lack of lighting in the control room continued into the corridor. Rebecca dragged Orson to the same stairwell the three had originally ascended to reach the control deck. She tentatively placed her hand on the door. She did not remove her hand in pain. With no sign of fire, she kicked it in. There were some minor flames dotting the railing going down. The bright light emanating from the decks below them were less encouraging.

Undeterred, Rebecca ascended the stairwell. Orson followed, careful not to place his hand on the railing. He tried not to look down into the inferno, but it didn't matter. He could hear a contingent of Kan-ur's guards down in the pit. They were alive. Their armor protected them initially from the destruction of the flames around them, but only did so long enough to forestall immediate asphyxiation. Their screams mingled with the crackling of the fire to produce a noise ghastly enough to enervate Orson's will to survive. Rebecca's insistence alone got him out of the stairwell. Escaping from the inferno below them was easily the most anxiety-producing experience Orson Welles had endured in the last several minutes.

Rebecca and Orson emerged on another higher deck, thankful that it had some life left in it. The long, narrow deck appeared to extend the length of the ship. A series of ladders descended from circular hatches on the ceiling.

Rebecca climbed the first ladder, but stopped when she realized that the hatch was merely another porthole to the battle beyond.

"Damn. Don't need too many guesses as to where that one went," she remarked as she made her way up the second ladder.

"Where *what* one went?" Orson asked.

"The escape pod." Rebecca pulled the release valve to open the hatch above her.

"*Who* would have left in one?" Orson looked longingly back at the stairwell of death. His stomach felt increasingly heavy.

"Kan-ur. He lives." Rebecca's tone suggested no other answer was possible. "Climb up."

"Oh? Me? No, no. No, no, no. No," Orson yammered. Rebecca jumped down from the ladder to stare him down, but he was resolved to stand firm. "The last time you told me to climb aboard something, we crashed into *this* ship, and now we're on fire!"

Rebecca considered for a moment the arguments necessary to get him to move and decided she lacked the time. "Fine." She proceeded to complete the climb to the pod. "Good luck, Orson."

The door to the stairwell behind them blew off its hinges, replaced by a torrent of fire. The argument sufficiently won by a reprise of dying guards' screams, Orson climbed the ladder behind Rebecca.

The hatch sealed behind them without further action from Rebecca. The pod then exploded forth from the dying ship. Rebecca looked out each of the meager craft's three portholes.

"Do you see it?" she asked frantically.

"What?"

"The other pod!"

Orson tried to look out any of the windows Rebecca wasn't using, but all he could see were stars, the two larger ships, and the flashes of light between them. He suspected that was all she could see as well. To confirm his suspicions, Rebecca repeatedly slammed her hand against the distressingly feeble-looking walls of their lifeboat.

The two larger craft continued their volleys of fire toward one another, until the flaming, more damaged vessel broke apart at the seams. Three large chunks of the once-foreboding vessel fell to the earth below, its own energy now gone and unable to avoid the pull of the planet's gravity. Similarly ill-equipped to avoid an involuntary landing, their pod hit the atmosphere with increasing velocity.

\*　　\*　　\*

SUNDAY, OCTOBER 30, 1938
9:37 PM HAST
ITERATION 344
30 MILES OFF THE COAST OF OAHU, HAWAII

When an unidentified flying object crashes in the middle of the ocean, the United States of America breathes a sigh of relief. The alternative of a land-based event is a significantly trickier logistical nightmare. The thoroughly bewildered citizens of Woodstock, Illinois can attest to that much.

However, no one assigned to the Coastal Rescue Team out of Naval Station Pearl Harbor breathed easy tonight. Tracking little green men now adrift in the Pacific was anything but an ordinary task.

Open flames speckled the surface of the ocean as the

unit made it out to the crash site. The idle chatter that normally floated around during such a mission slowed when the assigned seamen realized the debris they encountered could not possibly be from any terrestrial aircraft.

This attitude about the work at hand maintained its low ebb until the general alarm rang out from the deck of the lead skiff. The Lieutenant in charge of that vessel moved to the fore of the craft.

"Why in the Hell are you making that Goddamn noise, seaman?" the Lieutenant asked.

The Midshipman handed his binoculars to the Lieutenant, and through them he saw a relatively undamaged white buoy in the water—far from any rational location for such a marker—with a single blinking light at the top of its hull.

The Lieutenant ordered his vessel to close in on the buoy, and bring it aboard. Every soul on board climbed to the deck to witness the unlikely sight. The Lieutenant commandeered an acetylene torch and approached the captured craft slowly while the others gawked at it from a distance. The men all thought the Lieutenant was terribly brave, wanting to be certain that whatever would happen to their small boat happened to him first. For his own part, the Lieutenant neglected to mention the true purpose of his initiative. If anyone made history on this boat, he was damned sure going to make sure he made it first.

"You suppose it's German?" an Ensign asked.

"What're ya, simple? Of course it's not German!" another sailor answered.

"That writing on the hull—it's in English," a third commented, unable to understand the implications of such a statement.

"Then who's attacking us?" asked the first.

"No one would bother attacking Pearl Harbor," the second snapped. "Hawaii's too remote."

"I heard they did a full blown attack drill at the base a few years back," the third commented. "The base's defenses crumbled like a cookie."

"Quiet!" the Lieutenant barked as he ignited the torch. The deck became a beacon of bright white light as the Lieutenant—who for that instance was second-guessing both his altruism and opportunism—inched closer to the buoy. He wondered if the object was actually just an American buoy that an errant wave from the crash of the larger vessel carried out this far. He only stopped the flame of the torch when one particular detail on the object struck him. An arrow pointed to a single, circular black mark on the buoy's surface. Above the arrow, in clear black was written "PRESS HERE."

So he did.

With a hiss, a panel with an area of roughly two square feet popped off the buoy's hull. The craft then secreted two figures. These figures were not diminutive, slimy creatures from the planet Venus, either. They were real people, not unlike those from the mainland, although they were dressed in garments woven out of tire rubber.

The first figure was a woman. She crawled out of the contraption and regarded the sailors that greeted her with almost no expression whatsoever. It was as if finding herself suddenly at sea had no bearing on the course of her life. The second was a man. He was young, but remarkably wild-eyed. He looked from sailor to sailor as if he were a newly canonized Saint approaching the Pearly Gates. He yelped with joy as he staggered around the deck. It was as if he were struggling to confirm whether they were truly there or not. The sound failed to shake the woman companion out of her stupor, and sounded vaguely to the Lieutenant like the voice of Doc Savage or some other pulp figure from the radio.

"Yes!" the man of the buoy offered when he finally found words. "Anchors aweigh, my boys! You, there! Admiral!"

"I'm a Lieutenant, Sir," the Lieutenant said, leery of the wild man now on his boat.

"And I've only found success in the theater and radio, but we must not limit our ambition, dear boy—"

"Orson..." the woman called out to the man, giving her first indication to those assembled on the boat that she was still alive.

"You must immediately radio your superiors, and they in turn must alert their own superiors with all available haste that a massive calamity will befall this planet within just a few—"

"Orson!" The woman cried out, and finally drew his attention. She pointed everyone's attention upward. A swarm of locusts soared overhead—although even a few of the sailors had the perspective to grasp that what filled the sky were actually, whole, fiercely operational versions of the felled craft around them. The man looked back down to his fellow traveler. She now pointed east, and every man on that boat looked to see a bright golden haze where the mainland should have been.

The light beyond them flashed bright green and the night returned, although an undercurrent of the green remained.

"It's too late," the woman said. Without exception, each of the sailors had no clue what was going on anymore.

\*    \*    \*

Orson and Rebecca followed the Lieutenant to the

bridge after the Deck Officer ran to his superior with a stricken expression that appeared to have nothing to do with the emerald sky.

The Lieutenant picked up the radio handset. The device crackled with a frantic cascade of desperate voices, each of which had lost all sense of proper radio decorum.

"It was even worse before I came to get you, skipper," the Deck Officer said in response to the Lieutenant's perplexed reaction. The signal reduced until it was gone, replaced by static.

The small boat tasked with investigating the crashed object immediately abandoned its mission and burned all available fuel to return to Naval Base Pearl Harbor as fast as possible. As it travelled, the bright green eastward horizon remained constant in the night sky, but another greenish tint grew in the sky to the west.

When they reached the base, all that remained of it—and, for that matter, the islands beyond—was on fire. The panic that filled the radio only minutes before now filled the boat. For his part, the Lieutenant had the boats comb along the beach, eventually finding a stretch of land that was less fire and more ash mingled with newly formed glass. They found no survivors in their search, but it was no worse a place than anywhere else to try to figure out what to do next.

Sailors screamed over sailors as the chain of command shared the same fate as the rest of society. Orson's voice was the only distinct sound in the cacophony. Rebecca regained strength in the minutes since the world ended, went back to the boat, and rummaged through the escape pod for any useful equipment.

She eventually returned to the grounded sailors carrying only a small aerosol can. She moved past them towards what was left of the beachhead. While Orson and the sailors continued their ultimately fruitless frittering, she began spraying the can on the surface of the sand. The can was a far more efficient version of the Lieutenant's bulky acetylene device. The conversation among the men halted at the sight of Rebecca walking up and down the beach, dragging sparks with her as she trotted.

Done with her work, Rebecca walked once again past the sailors. She held the aerosol can like a weapon. The sailors diverted from her path immediately, but Orson stayed where he was.

"What the hell was that?" Orson asked.

"A message."

"To whom?" Orson asked. He was following Rebecca as she made her way back to the pod.

"To the Rockettes," she said. "Who do you think?" She pointed up to the toxic sky. "It was a message to *him*."

"Well, since I'm fresh out of flying saucers from which I could view this message, do you care to indulge—?"

"In a minute," Rebecca told him. She turned back to the sailors. "Gentlemen, I'm going to need your attention for a moment!" They had all been staring directly at her since she first activated the can, but she continued.

"There is every reason to believe you dozen or so men are all that remain of not only the United States Armed Forces, but the United States as well.

"Terrible things are happening right now, and there is nothing we can do about it. However, there *will* be things we can do to the things responsible. I can assure you of that much.

"I've written a message into the beach that, when read by the people that did this, will strike fear into their hearts. I'm now going to re-name this boat with that same message, but let us get one thing abundantly clear before we continue: We—myself and Mr. Welles, here—are in charge. We've got a lot of work to do now, so anyone who has a problem with that new method of operation will be left on this beach to fend for themselves."

The men looked at each other. They remained motionless, as if waiting for some other order or development to either change their situation back to the status quo, or finally bring them to your doom.

"Thanks for your attention," Rebecca finally said, realizing she had offered nothing by way of a conclusion. She then nodded at Orson and proceeded to use torch to cross out the boat's decidedly unromantic call number. The sailors continued to mutter amongst themselves, but with decidedly less volume than before. When she finished her work, Orson could see both the message, and the name of their new home. The hull of the boat read:

#octobersurvives

Orson looked at Rebecca and the conclusion he had been fighting ever since the sky turned green became unavoidable. His theatrical career was over.

# CHAPTER SEVEN

SUNDAY, OCTOBER 30TH 1938
11:47 PM GMT
ITERATION 344
LOW EARTH ORBIT

Kan-ur found the quiet strangely soothing. He could see the green flames consuming the planet below outside the porthole of his escape pod. The Earth blazed in chaos, while from his safe cocoon all was calm; all was bright.

Assuming his people performed their duties to his specifications, the various leaders of that bright blue orb would be the first to die. Roosevelt, Churchill, Mussolini, Stalin, and even William Randolph Hearst met their end at the hands of highly coordinated advance assassination squads. The reasons Kan-ur included Hearst on that list were known only to him. It was no matter: the squad assigned to the newspaper magnate's death would quickly understand the need for urgency, but no one would believe those that survived the operation. As he had before, Kan-ur would keep Hitler around for a short while. He could always put such men to some use.

Kan-ur's feeling of serenity expanded with the knowledge that Orson Welles—both of them—had died as his former ship crashed on the planet below. As much as he hoped this was the last time the human race would have to go through the resettlement process, Kan-ur hoped even more that he would never see Orson Welles—*any* Orsons Welles—ever again.

Eventually, the womb-like silence Kan-ur enjoyed ceased, and one of the other vanguard ships retrieved his escape vehicle. When the hatch to the craft hissed open away from him and he faced a contingent of his own guards leveling their own weapons at him, for the briefest moment Kan-ur felt defeat. October's words to the people of Earth must have found their intended audience. Widespread revolt followed by an ignominious end would prove to be the only events to which Kan-ur could look forward.

The guards dropped their weapons without hesitation. Wordlessly, Kan-ur walked past the armed servants. His future was safe all along.

\*    \*    \*

The command crew of the vessel had clearly never dreamed they would have Chairman Kan-ur as a guest while the operation to settle the new Earth still raged. They were collectively unprepared for the stress or honor of their situation. Kan-ur couldn't possibly care what their feelings on the matter might be, just so long as they got through their report a little bit faster.

"Most of the fires around the planet will burn out within the next..." The Captain of the vessel looked up from the printed version of his information to confirm with his assistant. "Two? Yes, two hours. The ark ships are currently in parking orbit around Mars. Once the temporary shelters are operational in the various habitable zones, they will begin the repopulation procedures. We should have the larger structures up within the week."

"Disposal procedures?"

"Er—ah..." the captain stalled while his attaché handed him another tablet, displaying more raw data for his review. "Extermin—Disposal procedures are nearly complete. Those that have missed the larger enfilade are currently being rounded up. They'll be given the option to become productive members of society. In the event that they don't or decide to provide any other sort of resistance, well..."

"The outer zones will take care of them." Kan-ur didn't bother looking at the officer. "Yes, I know this. Is there anything in your report that I can't obtain from my own imagination?" He stared out the window and once again contemplated the fates of the various men named Welles.

When his inquiry was met with silence by the captain, Kan-ur let his fury begin to bubble to the surface. "Captain, if I am keeping you from more pressing duties, please inform me, and I will find someone that can tell me that which I need to hear."

Met with more silence, Kan-ur whipped around only to find the Captain looking agape at the information in front of him. "What is it?" Kan-ur asked. No panic infiltrated his voice. How could it? He had spent untold eons perfecting this one set of events. It was nearly impossible that something could go wrong *now*.

"Pull up Oahu," the Captain requested.

One of the technicians in the control room proceeded to carry out the order, but at a glacial pace. On one of the area's massive displays, a beachhead marred by dwindling fires gave way to a closer view of the same area. Someone had scorched the one message into the surface of the glassy sand that could fill Kan-ur with something akin to worry.

#octobersurvives

Kan-ur stared at the image of the Hawaiian sand for a full minute without saying another word. He shook furiously as he turned back to stare out the window. The officers present kept their distance.

*Which one?* he wondered.

\*　　\*　　\*

AUGUST 12, 1951
4:17 PM GMT
ITERATION 344
NEARLY THIRTEEN YEARS LATER
SOMEWHERE ALONG WHAT WAS ONCE THE ENGLISH COUNTRYSIDE
EARTH

"Lieutenant?"

"Yes, October?"

"Fire in the hole!"

The two men ran for the hills beyond as fast as they could. The exposure suits they wore to protect them from the radioactive waste spread over most of the planet made their escape a slow, sloshing process. Both the Lieutenant and October—that is, the newer October—were relieved to realize that they were still taking in air that was predominantly made up of oxygen when the blast from their incendiary device blew a ring of concussive force in all directions and knocked them supine onto the ground.

"There! Are you happy now, Jack?"

The Lieutenant's response came through the thick

cloud that currently surrounded them. "Why do you ask?"

"You're the one who wanted to use the larger payload," October replied. "With that much dynamite, we're liable to destroy the artifact before we find it."

When the dust settled the two friends—for nothing quite forges lasting friendships like barely missing out on the apocalypse—returned to the epicenter of their work. October shined a light in the chasm they created, periodically checking behind him to ensure that the native ghouls were not disturbed by their ruckus and making their way rapidly to their location for an impromptu supper. Just below the blast zone he could see ancient wooden support beams that indicated this area might have once been a tomb, but he found nothing further of value.

"Damn it," October lamented.

"There are plenty of other sites to check." The Lieutenant looked down the excavation site once more.

October once again realized he had yet to tell Lieutenant Jack—or anyone outside of Rebecca—the true nature of these seemingly random expeditions back to the main planet. For all the Lieutenant knew, the moment they found anything as interesting as a desiccated mouse corpse in one of these holes, their mysterious mission would be accomplished.

"Fewer and fewer with every trip. I wish the old man had bothered to tell us anything more useful about what we're looking for before he died."

"And just so I've got it straight, the old man is...?"

"Myself." October always hated admitting to that particular leap in the narrative. "I will tell you one thing for certain, if I'm ever confronted with myself from deep within my own past, I'll open up to him."

The desperate wailing of their radio interrupted their commiseration. The Lieutenant activated the device.

"October unit receiving you. Go ahead."

"Mayday, mayday!" the report came back. "Ship down in transit! Ship down in transit!"

October and the Lieutenant exchanged a wary glance. They lost ships all the time to Kan-ur's forces, but it hardly warranted breaking radio silence while they were conducting operations on Earth. The casualty report would just as easily wait for them when they returned to base.

October grabbed the radio. "What ship is down?"

"The *Oneida II.*"

*       *       *

AUGUST 13, 1951
2:03 AM COORDINATED MARTIAN TIME
OCTOBER BASE BETA
THE ASTEROID BELT

The information October and Lieutenant Jack received on their trip back home only caused further confusion. There was plenty of risk in making a return trip Marsward so quickly after an incident like the one that appeared to destroy Rebecca's vessel. The information presented to them after they arrived offered no clarification.

October rubbed his temples after they watched the flight recorder from the missing ship. The rest of October's inner circle chattered away, expounding on various theories as to what may have befallen Rebecca and the *Oneida II.*

"S.B.?" October finally asked. The rest of those assembled immediately went silent. "Please show me the flight recorder footage once more."

The ever-helpful computer program nodded with a smile. "You bet! I'll get right on that. And, may I say, I sure am sorry about the loss of the ship..."

With no one pushing the digital assistant back to his task, S.B. took the hint better than October had ever seen the strange ghost do before. The main status display in their command center gave way to the same footage they had already watched twice. The interior of Rebecca's ship appeared as it proceeded on its course towards a raid on one of Kan-ur's power production plants *cum* pollution vomiters. Nothing seemed out of the ordinary, and then instantly POOF! The flight recorder ceased. They had no indication that any remnant of the ship was near its last known location. It was as if the ship had never existed in the first place.

"Were there any enemy ships in the area at the time?" October asked.

S.B. processed the request and searched his databases. The program manifested this process across S.B.'s face as a serious look of contemplation. The "search face," as October had come to call it, always unnerved the hell out of him.

"None anywhere near the area, no. Intelligence reports indicate at the time that most enemy forces were scouring the surface of the planet looking for your expedition."

"It can't have just disappeared," October remarked. The others resumed their chattering, offering wild suggestions that had no basis in reality. As their talk continued, October felt the dull throbbing that accompanied him from Earth explode into a migraine radiating pain down his jaw. He slammed the conference table they all sat around. "Kan-ur must have developed a new weapon that can perform the feat we just witnessed. As of this moment, any pretense to safety that we have laid claim to before has officially ceased. I will make that bastard *pay*."

\*     \*     \*

WEDNESDAY, OCTOBER 19TH 1938
9:37 PM CST
ITERATION 345
WOODSTOCK, ILLINOIS
THE MERCURY DINER
EARTH

Orson Welles hung up the phone and took position at one of the tables in the establishment.

"What'll it be?" the waitress asked.

"Pie."

"We only have rhub—"

"I don't care," Orson said. She went to fetch his order, leaving him alone with his thoughts, at least until Roger Hill and his unique brand of gentle disapproval arrived.

A dull buzzing introduced itself into the back of Orson's mind. The motion gave way to an even more alarming outward vibration that knocked a wrapped set of silverware off the table and onto the ground. The phenomenon spread, and shook a pot of coffee off the counter. The container shattered on the ground.

Orson looked up from the table and saw the street outside of the diner fill with green light. Compulsion moved him outside the door, while the better part of reason fought the idea of German or Japanese mechanisms of death descending upon Illinois. As he looked up into the night sky, the diffuse illumination that had pulled him from the booth coalesced into a single tracking light on a solitary—yet impossible—flying craft. When the ship made contact with the asphalt of Main Street, the light deactivated. Orson looked around, but it still appeared as if he were the only man on Earth to see this particular sight.

With the normal illumination of street lamps guiding him, Orson walked towards the craft, which appeared to be named "Oneida III." Somehow the Greek designation for the vessel brought Orson some degree of comfort.

A panel on the craft hissed open. A dark silhouette stood within the newly-formed doorway. Preparing to be the first human to meet a man from Jupiter, Orson squinted at the figure. When he could get a clear look, disappointment followed. The figure was broad shouldered, and had a short-cropped, military style haircut. He had neither green skin, nor any other exaggeration in his appearance that might have made him a creature from a pulp novel. He might have been any number of older military men one might encounter on any ordinary day.

"Orson Welles!" the seemingly human creature left no room for inquiry in his voice.

Before Orson could answer, the figure approached him quickly and manhandled him on board the craft. "Yes! Who the hell are you?"

"Just call me 'Lieutenant'," the figure responded. "That's all you need to know."

\*　　\*　　\*

THURSDAY, DECEMBER 12, 1996
1:15 PM COORDINATED MARTIAN TIME
ITERATION 344
KAN-UR'S FLAGSHIP
MARTIAN ORBIT

October attempted to bring his sword down upon Kan-ur's frame with more fury than he might have previously thought his 81-year-old body could hold. Kan-ur shot forth with a lightning-fast parry and subsequent attack.

October could barely offer a defense that maintained his footing.

"If I wanted a kiss, I would have called your girlfriend," Kan-ur said as he slowly moved October into a corner. "What was her name, again?"

October's infirmity, lack of preparation and palpable anger got the better of him. Kan-ur took the final advantage. With one thrust, Kan-ur pushed his blades into October's sternum. He spread the two weapons for just a moment to ensure he filled his nemesis' final moments were with as much pain as possible.

Kan-ur took the moment of tragic confusion to set the ship's self-destruct protocol and make his escape from the control deck. The Lieutenant might have been able to catch up to the chairman, if he hadn't immediately tended to the fallen October.

"What are your orders?" the Lieutenant asked.

October felt his throat fill with warmth, and only some distant part of his mind determined the substance to be a vital amount of blood. "You should have gone after him, you damned fool!"

The Lieutenant turned to follow through on the order, but he croaked another admonition. "It's too damned late!"

October reached for the young Orson Welles, who remained cocooned in his own shock. Praying that he could somehow bring some measure of comfort to October's last moments in this life, the Lieutenant pushed the young man towards the audience he so desperately wanted to avoid. October focused his rapidly dimming strength on Orson arm.

"You must—" October attempted, then punctuated the half-formed thought with a gurgle that made Orson want to pull away more. "I should have—"

And the performance ended. October was dead. Long

live October.

\*　　\*　　\*

SUNDAY, OCTOBER 30, 1938
9:18 PM CST
ITERATION 345
JUST OUTSIDE MANHATTAN, KANSAS
EARTH

The Lieutenant jumped out of the escape pod the instant it hissed open. Weapon already drawn, he ran out into the cornfield in hopes that there was something that still could be done—

—only to be greeted by bright green haze illuminating the sky to the west, south, and east. He spent only the briefest moment wondering about the younger version of himself currently burning alive in Hawaii. He then looked back to Orson, still cowering in the small emergency craft.

Click.

"You have five seconds to tell me where the Hell you came from before it's not going to matter one bit," the farmer said from behind his quivering rifle.

The Lieutenant raised his own weapon and before the farmer could react, his more advanced firearm discharged. The farmer threw his red-hot gun into the air.

"I don't want to hurt you," the Lieutenant pleaded. "But the only chance you have to survive is if you follow us north. Do you understand?"

The farmer said nothing. The only sound between them was the whimpering of the farmer's nearby daughter, no older than three.

"We don't want to hurt you. Isn't that right, Orson?"

The new, young October yelped a reply and shrugged.

\*     \*     \*

WEDNESDAY, OCTOBER 19TH, 1938
9:37 PM CST
ITERATION 346
WOODSTOCK, ILLINOIS
THE MERCURY DINER
EARTH

"I'll have the pie."

"You know it's rhub—"

One by one, the windows of the diner shattered inward. The waitress immediately hit the deck, while Orson remained stuck in his booth. He had nowhere to go while Germany made their opening gambit in a small town sixty-two miles outside of Chicago.

Two large men adorned in shiny black leather uniforms stormed into the diner.

"Are you Orson Welles?" the lead soldier asked.

*Have these men seen me on the stage?* Orson briefly wondered as he let a slight affirmation escape his lips. Before such an admission could coalesce into actual words, the men quickly ushered him out of the establishment.

\*     \*     \*

They moved quickly through the town streets. If their leader's plans were to come to fruition, not a single moment could be wasted.

"Where the Hell are you people taking me?" Orson stopped walking. "If Housey sent you, I'll tell you goons right now, I'm a member of Equity."

"Please step lively, sir," the lead guard ordered and

pushed him forward. "Everything will be explained in due ti—"

Orson yelped as his foot snagged on a pothole in the street beyond. He fell forward before the other men could react. A wet thwack echoed through Woodstock as the lead guard dropped to his knees to investigate Orson's injuries. He pulled Orson up from the ground. It took more effort than he might have previously thought to move their charge. A chunk of the damaged concrete had wedged itself into Orson's skull.

"Oh..." the lead guard brought his hand up from Orson's neck. The appendage was covered in dark red blood that gave off only the dimmest hints of crimson in the street light's glow. "He's dead."

The other guard twitched with panic. "Kan-ur will kill us! What do we do?"

"Run!" the lead guard resolved. The two men charged with bringing Orson Welles to Kan-ur during this iteration were never heard from again.

*   *   *

FRIDAY, JUNE 19TH, 1992
1:02 PM COORDINATED MARTIAN TIME
ITERATION 345
OCTOBER BASE GAMMA
THE ASTEROID BELT

"You can close the feed, S.B."

October spent the first two decades of his life supremely confident that he would not be an outside observer to his own death. Now he had the unique experience of viewing his own dead body for the second time.

It felt morbid to ship the young man's body back to Mars and forward through time, but the piercing logic of the act cut through any emotional qualms October may have had about the idea. He had to survive, especially if they were unable to stop Kan-ur this time. A nearly complete set of perfect transplant organs wouldn't be a bad thing to have around.

October tapped his hand across the table, lost in thought. "Now that I really think about it," he said to his people. "I suppose I should have—"

The ground shook beneath him. The thought scattered to the back of his mind where it would eventually all but evaporate.

"All right, everyone!" October called out. "You know what this means!"

The battle had begun anew.

\*     \*     \*

SATURDAY, NOVEMBER 12TH, 1955
10:04 PM EST
ITERATION 346
OLYMPUS HQ
MANHATTAN, NEW YORK
EARTH

If Kan-ur ignored the rapidly depleting resources at his disposal, he had a great deal to celebrate. October had long since lost both the battle and the war. Truly, there was little left of the old fool's forces that could mount any sort of serious interference. The only matter that remained for Kan-ur was to finally ensure humanity's survival and supremacy once and for all.

"Shall we take precautions, Lord Chairman?" the call

inquired from speakers positioned all around Kan-ur.

"Not at all. October has been instrumental in the formation of our society. Doesn't matter if he did so largely against his will. It would be rude to not grant him an audience."

The main door to Kan-ur's study hissed open. Normally, a contingent of his most skilled guards stood watch beyond the doorway. The moment Kan-ur received word that October's forces sprung a last-ditch raid on his headquarters, his amusement left no course of action other than to give those brave men the night off.

The man trying to invade his inner sanctum was hardly a threat. Not anymore, at least.

The intruder inched forward, looking as if the two small steps would fell him long before any guards might have had the chance. Stone-white eyes looked out from a nearly hairless, supremely wrinkled head. October once relied on a cane to assist his mobility, but the increasing infirmity of time necessitated augmenting his limbs with rudimentary cybernetic enhancements. Even his replacement parts were past their warranty.

"You came for me *alone*?" Kan-ur asked.

"Bah!" October's voice was barely above a whisper. "Doesn't matter if I came with every one of your goons on my side, or not at all. I'm not sure you can die, you bastard."

For a moment, Kan-ur considered unsheathing his cranial blades. He decided that cleaning his weapons after the encounter would not be worth it. Kan-ur simply moved towards the old man, pushing him against the nearest wall. Instead of grunting in resistance to the attack, October merely wheezed at its inevitability. Kan-ur felt the crack of several ribs under the relatively slight force of his push.

"Then why come at all? Why not accept your fate?"

Kan-ur slightly released some of his pressure on October. "Don't you see that this is a kindness I do for you?"

The grey-clouded eyes of his old nemesis focused on him, despite their inability to see much. "You're so sure that everything you do is for the greater good, that there is no way your murderous, warped sense of righteousness can possibly be overcome." If Kan-ur didn't know better that the man in front of him was quickly dying, it would have sounded as if October laughed. "I came here to say only one thing."

Kan-ur leaned in.

"You better be *damned* sure."

*　*　*

SUNDAY, OCTOBER 16TH, 1938
8:37 PM EST
ITERATION 347
MANHATTAN, NEW YORK
JUST OUTSIDE THE NEW AMSTERDAM THEATRE

"I think I have notes for an adaptation of *Jekyll and Hyde*," Howard Koch said while Orson Welles attempted to make an escape from the ambulance.

"The New Amsterdam!" The driver called out.

"Then *Jekyll and Hyde* it is," Orson called out behind him. His embarrassment at the hands of the RKO studio chief was a distant memory. His boredom with this Housey-mandated conversation had taken all precedence.

That boredom was then in turn superseded by irritation that Houseman couldn't even bother to offer a feeble retort. Orson turned to consider them as an errant cloud cast a shadow over the walkway leading up to the theater... despite the fact that nightfall should have more than accounted for any darkness, and shadows had no place here.

Housey and Koch's agape stares did nothing to aid Orson's confusion. He turned back around to witness the slow descent of a smooth, black aircraft. Green energy flowed through the airship's hull.

A hatch slid open. A single man—human? German, he had to be German—exited and walked straight towards Orson. He carried a large sword that appeared to glimmer with its own inherent source of power.

"Orson Welles?" the man asked.

"That's me." Any other form of distraction Orson would have assumed was due to Housey's machinations, but the sheer perfection of this tableau led Orson to believe that it just might be real.

The man started to hand Orson the sword.

"This belongs to you," the man said, although he almost immediately jerked the object from Orson's grasp. "I'm instructed to show you this first." The man reached into a bag slung from his shoulder and pulled out a thin slate of polished black glass. He placed his thumb against the underside of the object just as they all heard the distant sound of sirens approaching. The object, too, glowed with its own source of power, and reverse projected an image of an old man.

"Orson Welles," the man in the glass began. "I have neither the time nor the inclination to spell out what is happening to you. I'm you. You're me. And terrible things are on their way to your location right now.

"Don't believe me? Take the sword which should be available to you now."

The man from the ship insistently held the weapon towards Orson once more. Playing along, Orson grabbed the weapon...

...and everything became clear...

Orson turned back to the man on the glass.

"Now that I have your attention, young man," the man Orson now knew to call October said, "I have one other thing to say to you before you take on your destiny: I should have trusted you."

The image of October blinked away, and yet Orson somehow knew the old man's name was now his own. He looked to the small crowd unable to take their eyes away from him. He looked above and saw that the sky began to glow a soft shade of green.

"You there!" the new October called out to the Pilot he had just met. "We need to get as many people as we can onto this vessel."

The Pilot started ushering people on board, but stopped at Housey and Koch. "Even these two, October?"

October hesitated as he looked at Housey. "Yes?" There was barely enough time to save anyone. He had to save as many as he could, though. Including Housey.

# INTERLUDE

SATURDAY, OCTOBER 21, 2215
4:17 PM COORDINATED MARTIAN TIME
ITERATION 1
OLYMPUS INSTITUTE DORMITORY FACILITIES
OLYMPUS MONS, MARS

The Scientist's miracle never came. He spent the next several years quietly pursuing his theories regarding time travel and its applications for mankind, although he made a point of never again bringing up the idea in front of people.

Circumstances on Mars continued to grow worse over the intervening years, so much so that the Institute might have been more open to the idea in the second decade of the twenty-third century. They were certainly more open to the ridiculous notion of searching high and low for the famed October Archive. They also pursued the Sisyphean task of somehow re-terraforming Earth to the point where it would magically be free of pollution, strife, or any sort of relationship to the idea of cause and effect.

The Scientist also branched out into ideas he would have scoffed at only a few years ago. When the

Chairwoman's Chief Aide indicated that the only thing separating reality from the Scientist's ideas was an old-fashioned miracle, his remarks stung. Their close proximity with reality was to blame. This unfortunate truth weighed the Scientist down each day he arrived at the office, he found himself no longer lamenting the unlikelihood of a miracle, but instead hoping to find one.

A quest to find little green men would be a herculean task without the full resources of the Institute behind him. With every fifteen-minute increment of access to the Olympus Institute's vast satellite array, he pointed the device towards Alpha Centauri and sent one word in every possible language, including binary:

Help.

He knew Alpha Centauri would provide no answer. If the closest Solar System possessed intelligent life—unlikely to the point of absurdity—the odds that those far-flung star people possessed sufficiently advanced technology to both break the few elements of Einsteinian physics that still limited FTL travel *and* save humanity from their own self-destruction was enough to move past quantum probability and into the theoretical realm of the impossible.

The Scientist considered petitioning the Institute to allow construction of a deep space probe to carry a distress call beyond their quiet corner of the Milky Way, but this never got past consideration and into action.

Even he didn't believe that such a move was an option. If intelligent life existed beyond those beings that had left the Earth, they were certain to be a rarity.

The air seemed suddenly thin to the Scientist as he contemplated these harsh realities in his small living quarters not far from the Institute's main campus. He only snapped out of his dark reverie when the telephone application on his watch shuddered with a cadence that brought even more wonderful news than the prospects for the second end of the world:

Work was calling, and on a Saturday, no less.

"What?" the Scientist barked into his device. His career may have been stuck in perfect stasis, but his tenure had obvious privileges.

The line disconnected as a pounding on the front door echoed throughout the living room. The Scientist let his arm drop to his side, and he went to answer his uninvited visitor.

He nearly closed the door again when he realized the caller was none other than the Chairwoman's Chief Aide. He took what little comfort he could out of the knowledge that he was just as stuck as the Scientist, but bristled as the Aide proved twice as difficult to get rid of. The Aide looked harried and tired—he always looked like that—but the lack of a self-satisfied smirk gave him an air of deadly earnestness.

"There's been an accident," the Aide said. "Get your things and come with me."

The Scientist didn't budge. "What kind of an accident?"

The Aide had already moved on to the next living unit in an effort to ruin *that* Institute staffer's weekend. He turned back to the Scientist, annoyed at the need to do so. "Massive seismic event at the canals."

The Scientist figured that was the reason the air around him had thinned out so suddenly. If the power to any of the life support systems became taxed due to a sudden sheering force, the whole system tended to have a period of brownouts. It was a wonderful way to live. "I'm not a seismologist."

"You went to *college*, though, right?" the Aide asked. The question quickly morphed into a statement as he made good on his threat and moved on to the next door. "It's all hands on deck."

The Scientist briefly considered further arguing against his usefulness in this scenario. Instead he angrily grabbed his jacket and wondered why anyone still used the term "all hands on deck" when the last sea vessel had come into port hundreds of years and an entire planet ago.

\*　　\*　　\*

By the time they arrived at the canals, there was nothing that a scientist—any sort of scientist—could do for the victims of the "accident." However, the Scientist's superiors were not about to let media coverage of this tragedy not include the line "experts from the Olympus Institute were on hand to provide assistance." And so, the Scientist was on hand to witness the horror.

Bodies—men, women, and children alike—were brought into the makeshift hospital on the outskirts of the canals. They all suffered from some variation of third degree burns. When he glanced at the grim sight, he didn't notice any immediate signs of asphyxiation or other indications of exposure to the unfiltered Martian atmosphere. Additionally, not one of the victims had expired as a result of blunt force trauma. Even though the Scientist wasn't remotely a medical doctor, he couldn't help but notice that none of his observations pointed to any sort of seismic—he felt silly referring to anything as a "marsquake"—activity.

"What kind of—" the Scientist struggled once again on the universally accepted term as he stopped one of the emergency relief workers. "What happened here?"

"Haven't they told you people?" the Worker snapped at the Scientist as she sealed shut a tragically minuscule body bag. The Scientist thought she might have had a different attitude if his jumpsuit and credentials didn't include a large representation of the magenta-hued Olympus emblem.

She softened, although it felt more like pity than compassion. "Massive electrical discharge." She then attempted to move on with her own helpless quest.

The Scientist took a lurching step towards the worker, nearly tripping in the process. "What did you say?"

"Electrical discharge, from somewhere deep in the planet's core. Fried the whole settlement."

The Scientist heard a dull buzzing as he fell to the ground. Amid the sheer tonnage of death about which he could do nothing, he laughed loud enough to draw attention to himself.

The reaction of others didn't matter. If the planet's core held that much energy, he may have just found his miracle.

# CHAPTER EIGHT

WEDNESDAY, OCTOBER 19, 1938
9:37 PM CST
ITERATION 349
THE MERCURY DINER
WOODSTOCK, ILLINOIS
EARTH

Orson Welles hung up the telephone and turned back to the counter. The old man sitting at one of the booths continued to eye him, but Orson chose to ignore it. The seething contempt with which the other occupant of the booth looked at Orson reinforced the wisdom of that decision.

The waitress brought Orson his pie and promptly returned to her previous work. Confronted with the reality of rhubarb, he sighed in disgust but proceeded undeterred. The old man laughed at his pie-related difficulties.

"Anything for an audience," Orson told the old man. He included just enough irritation to illustrate his hope that the conversation ended there.

"Mr. Welles, might I be able to buy you a cup of

coffee, sir?" The old man interrupted Orson's train of thought.

Orson diverted at the last moment from re-sitting upon the counter stool to consider the odd pair who were the only other patrons of the diner. It briefly occurred to Orson that the two might have recognized him from his various stage credits, but deep down he had a hard time believing anyone outside of Manhattan's elite would know his face.

"You appear to know me, but you have me at a disadvantage, sir," Orson said to the old man.

"That's certainly one way of putting it," the Old Man said as Orson approached the table. "Please, sit."

"Why?" Orson kept his distance from the table.

The Old Man and his companion regarded each other for a long moment, before the old man finally looked straight at Orson and sighed.

"Well, I am you. My name was once Orson Welles, and I'm from what you would call the future."

Amusement alone forced Orson to finally sit across from his two new friends as the waitress approached. She handed the old man a menu. "This sounds like the beginning of an H.G. Wells novel."

"Well, future is a bit of a misnomer. In truth, I'm from a parallel dimension, the 7th such reality to be victim of a temporal incursion from an extra-terrestrial known as Kan-ur. The difference is academic."

"I'll let you folks look at the menu a bit longer," the waitress said to the geriatric prankster. She scurried back to her cleaning.

"I suppose you're my *fee marraine*?" Orson asked the old man's companion.

"No," the companion said. His tone matched his scowl.

"There will be time for more detailed answers later," the Old Man said. "For the time being, young man, you must simply trust me and come with us."

Orson laughed and checked behind him, either in hopes that Roger Hill had arrived or Housey had suddenly developed something approximating a sense of humor and had produced his way into this farce. Orson was not so lucky; he was all alone.

"Trust you, 'Mr. Welles'?" Orson asked.

"It's your dying wish, I assure you. And you may call me October. I stopped using your name a long time ago."

"October?" Orson asked.

"Yes," the Old Man replied.

"That's one hell of a mysterious name," Orson remarked. "It's also a bit hackneyed, no?"

"You may come to like it."

"I'm actually meeting someone," Orson said as he attempted to exit their booth. "But I do want to thank you both for the strangest conversation I could have ever hoped for."

He moved back towards the counter, silently considering the option of waiting for Hill outside of the diner. "You're waiting for Roger Hill, headmaster of the former Todd School for Boys."

Orson stopped and turned to the two strange diners. "Former?"

"You've been gone too long," October replied.

"If you know who I am, you know who Roger is. That is hardly clairvoyance that you're displaying," Orson said, although his words were suddenly unsure.

"Yes," October admitted. "But would I know what Hill told you when your father died in a sea of his own drink? 'He may not have been much of a man or a father, but he did have something to do with the man you will become.'"

Orson looked at October. If this were some sort of elaborate joke, it had become so perfectly hurtful that he could no longer see the punchline.

"I also wouldn't be able to tell you that I—you, that is—have a scar on your left knee." October rose from his seat and put weight on a gleaming metal cane.

"Everyone does," Orson dismissed the observation. "I once worked as a fortune teller in Ireland—"

"—and you realized that nearly everyone has a scar on their left knee, and would be able to impress them with your mental powers if you remarked upon it."

Orson took a step towards October.

"Give us five minutes, Mr. Welles. If we don't have you convinced by then, this can be just another story you repeatedly tell people."

"They would never believe me."

"They don't believe your stories now."

When Roger Hill finally arrived at the Mercury Diner nearly twenty minutes later, the place was fresh out of its once plentiful supply of Orsons Welles. He didn't think much of the young man's disappearance. Orson Welles had flaked out on him countless times before and would turn up again before too long.

\* \* \*

"Mind the gap in the pavement," October said as the three moved quickly down Main Street.

"What? Why?" Orson asked after already stumbling on the gap in question.

"A quarter of an inch to the right and you would have cracked your head open," said October's companion, who eventually identified himself by the name of Reilly Goodman.

"I really don't need a mother."

"No," October interjected. "He's quite serious. A few iterations ago you perished back on that street corner. Made an awful mess of things."

"If you ask me, it's given us our one chance to put things the way they ought to be," Goodman said.

October grunted in near-approval.

"Listen, I just—" Orson began.

They rounded a corner and were confronted with a floating hunk of glowing, polished metal the size of a large truck. The object was breathtaking, and almost Germanic in its unnerving purity. Had Orson possessed the ability to think beyond his shock at the sight, he might have concluded October and Goodman came from a world that possessed such machines for decades or maybe centuries. This craft was engineering perfected.

"Coming with us?" Goodman asked as he walked and the old man hobbled their way past Orson.

Orson looked behind him. He figured Roger Hill would never begrudge him the opportunity to pursue this hallucination to its conclusion.

*　　*　　*

FRIDAY, OCTOBER 25, 1985
4:13 PM COORDINATED MARTIAN TIME
ITERATION 348
OCTOBER BASE GAMMA
ASTEROID 1138, THE ASTEROID BELT

October and Goodman's ship, the *Oneida V*, had the advantage of a head start as they emerged from the Martian Gate and returned to their base built into the core of Asteroid 1138. The favorable situation did not end there.

That their base was a needle not just in a haystack but a large pile of nearly identical needles served to stymie Kanur's attempts to locate them.

Orson's befuddled expression at his surroundings, and his absolute incredulity at video screen depictions of flying cars and the futuristic cityscape back on the Earth of 1985 was consistent in any reality. When he saw an ornate portrait of John Houseman hanging in the corridors of this place, any semblance of plausibility was lost. The brass plaque that read "NEVER FORGET" captivated him.

"Ah, yes," October remarked when he realized what had so enraptured his younger self's attention. "It turned out he was one hell of a warrior."

"It's like I'm in hell." Orson's remark was meant more about the painting than anyone else.

"No, Hell still awaits," October said. "Please come, time is short."

"If I'm to believe what is happening, time is the only non-combustible resource in all of creation."

October didn't argue with him but continued to usher him along.

"So this Kan-ur kills all of the world's leaders first?" Orson asked once it became clear he would get no further information as to how Housey had become a space-age Jean Valjean. The journey into the future and out beyond the Red Planet had afforded October the opportunity to impart a substantial sum of needed information, even if it was merely the tip of the mighty sword to follow.

"And Hearst," October clarified. They made their way through the corridor connecting the hangar and the rest of the facility. "Actually killing Hearst is usually the first order of business during each of their invasions. It has to be."

"Why?" Orson asked.

"We can't tell you."

"That's only going to spike my curiosity."

"I imagine it would," October replied as they reached the end of the corridor. They passed through the doors and into the first main chamber of the facility. The room seemed far less committed to the coordination of one single effort and more like a dental school. Technicians and soldiers—all lean and hungry but far from starving nor desperate—milled about. A single metal chair occupied the center, with every single action, soul, and electrical cord focusing on the seat.

One of the technicians approached the three arrivals. "The chair is ready," the worker told October while eyeing Orson with something between deep suspicion and unnerving hero worship.

"How are the navigation metrics?" Goodman asked the technician.

The technician snapped his attention to Goodman. "The chairman appears to be searching for us much closer to low Mars orbit, just as we predicted. It will take them quite a bit of time to find us, even if they committed all of their resources to the endeavor, although..."

"Although?" Goodman asked.

"I haven't checked in with them in over an hour," the technician replied.

Goodman was already off and running towards the next chamber of the asteroid base when he said, presumably to October, "If you'll excuse me."

The technician returned back to his work. This left October to gesture for Orson to approach the chair.

"I beg your pardon?" Orson asked.

October patted the seat of the chair. "It won't bite." October then regarded the chair closely. "In truth, I have no idea what this process will do to you. Biting seems improbable." He patted the chair again. "Up you go."

Understanding that to distrust the source of his instructions might be unwise, if not self-defeating, Orson lowered himself into the chair. He couldn't shake the feeling that relenting to the old man's will might also prove to be a poor decision.

"What is this contraption?" Orson asked as one of the technicians strapped him into the device. Along with the metal clamps at his extremities, the technician attached plastic sensors to his forehead, shoulders and chest. October kept his distance from the entire affair. It only served to reinforce Orson's trepidation.

"Time runs short for everyone," October finally replied from his safe vantage point. It was as if he had already experienced what was about to happen to Orson, and knew he wanted no part of it. "Suffice it to say, if we are to be successful in saving the human race, you are going to need to process an obscene amount of information very quickly. This machine you're currently developing a profound connection with is a rudimentary mental implanter. Every school child back on Earth receives the half-baked propaganda that passes for education these days via similar—if far more refined—devices. Basic education takes a week of hour-long sessions. You, my young friend, are a once-in-a-generation mind—"

"You flatter me, sir," Orson interjected. The compliment lost some potency coming from himself.

"Yes, but you also have the emotional maturity of an infant," October spat in response. The air between the two men turned sour. Even the technicians stopped their work.

"I apologize." October didn't look at Orson when he offered the apology. It was meant far more for the others than for Orson. He then turned back to the young man. "If I may continue?"

Orson intended to make a submissive gesture towards

the Old Man, but with his head securely fastened to a hard surface, the expression resembled a violent twitch.

"Your mind is unique," October clarified, but immediately changed directions when he could no longer ignore his word choice. "Well, your brain is certainly unusual, and it has the added virtue of youth.

"You see, Mist—*Orson*, in order to be the one to not only save the future, but every possible future for humanity, you will need to know lifetimes of information, and we have no more than six hours to do so before this facility is nothing more than a cloud of dust indistinguishable from the rest of the asteroid belt.

"In order to do this—" October slowly made his way closer to Orson, his cane clicking against the floor. "—we will need a massive source of electronic information and an even more massive capacitor of power."

October held his cane and gazed at it. He depressed a small button near the top curve of the stick. A long blade sprang out of the tail end. The newly formed weapon appeared to glimmer independently of any light source.

"Luckily enough, the object I have in my hand should provide both in abundance."

"What is it?"

"It's—" October began as he considered the blade he had now brought close to his face. "It's a sword, or at least it was when I found it. Circumstances are such that I've had to hide it in plain sight."

"Where did you find it?"

"I'm..." October continued to consider the sword and appeared to drift away with only some vague memory to accompany him. "I'm not going to lie to you," he finally said when he looked at Orson again.

"You won't lie to me. But you aren't going to tell me, either."

October nodded, if a little stiffly. He once again defaulted to a steely, impenetrable expression. "Why tell you, my friend, when I can show you?" October then leveled the weapon at his younger counterpart.

Up until that moment, some degree of foolish pride mandated Orson not complain about the tightness of his restraints. Now, as he faced the possibility of being run through by himself, he twitched and flailed uselessly against them.

"Calm down," October assured him, but did not lower the weapon. Machinery worked behind Orson as he could see a small platform rise out of the floor. The otherwise smooth surface of the protrusion was interrupted by a hole not much larger than a key hole. "I have no idea what killing you might do to me. You can rest assured that I don't want to find out."

With his weapon raised, October moved to the platform.

"Will this hurt?" Orson asked once he ceased his resistance.

October stopped again. He considered the sword one final time. "I have no idea," he remarked, and then looked earnestly at Orson. "This is the first time anyone has ever tried it. I can't imagine it will be pleasant."

Orson wanted to form another question, even if he knew October was content to reveal no further information to him. He just didn't want that sword to go in the platform before—

—the old man jammed the weapon into the device—

\*    \*    \*

—and everything became clear.

Before Orson's eyes, he saw the Earth. It was bright

blue, much as he first saw it from space only a few short hours ago. It then grew dark. Bolts of lightning cracked across his vision.

Then, with a flash, it was blue green again. A swarm of what looked to be jet-black gnats engulfed the world, and it grew dark again.

This process transpired dozens, even hundreds of times before Orson's eyes before...

Before Orson felt all of the details of these images seep into every crevasse of his mind.

And before...

Before he felt a potent thrill at the sight of the decay.

Before he needed the decay.

Before he saw it as the only way forward.

Before the guilt at his own complicity with the death surrounding him grew too much for him to bear.

And before he finally saw how it would all end.

\*    \*    \*

Orson woke with a start. His throat felt drier than he ever thought a part of his body could before, and yet his brow was slick with sweat. Despite the dim lighting around him, Orson could sense that his surroundings were the same dark-grey metal that passed for cement in this rabbit hole he found himself in, although the room feebly tried to cover its industrial origins by making use of magnificent decorations and opulent furniture. He also sensed...

"My friend?" The voice called out from the shadows. October was the source of the voice, but for the first few moments after the fog started to lift, Orson swore it had been a coat rack speaking to him. He spent a moment wondering if the response came from within.

"How long have I been asleep?" Orson asked.

"Not quite an hour."

"Really?" It felt impossibly longer.

"Initially, you made a serious attempt to kill every man, woman, and child in this facility," October told him. Were Orson not still so exhausted, he might have expressed something akin to shock. "Everyone felt a nap was in order. How do you feel now?"

"I feel—" Orson began. He paused for a moment to resist his first answer, but failed. "I feel as if you used a piece of cosmic material originating from the moment of the Big Bang as a capacitive data module—"

"—to implant you with the memories of every man to have the name Orson Welles in every single universe created by Kan-ur's travels through time?" With the amount of information swimming around the young man's head, it might have been October's final opportunity to help fill in Orson's gaps.

"Yes," Orson agreed. "This will sound quite mad," although he already knew it wouldn't. "But I also feel as if my mind—my very soul—has been akin to a giant porcelain plate. Now the plate has shattered, but each shard is the same size as the orig—"

"Fascinating," October interjected through his regret at asking the question.

The lights in the room came up. October approached the bed. Orson was surprised to feel his eyes adjust to the light without much pain. "I'd ask where that sword has been," Orson said. "But I think you know better than anyone that I already know."

"What, this?" October asked as he raised what was left of his cane. The wood concealing the weapon within had apparently incinerated under the stress of the procedure. Only a scorched, mangled strip of unremarkable metal remained of the blade. October tossed the object on a cabinet near Orson where it landed with a dull thud. "Then tell me. I'm curious myself."

"Well, it's—" Orson suddenly stopped. It was as if one of his aforementioned shards disappeared, and the only trace of its existence was an insistent feeling it never existed in the first place. "It's..." he tried again, with no better result to show for it. "I don't remember."

"That's not entirely surprising—"

"But I still remember where you and the others found it!" Orson's tone was frantic.

"And where would that be?"

"Why in the to—" The word evaporated in his mouth before he fully said it. He had never forgotten what he was going to say in the middle of uttering a particular word; he couldn't think of anyone who would experience such a deficit in faculties. A piece of information was either remembered or forgotten. It couldn't be both. And yet, the word had vanished from his mind. Tonsils? Tomato? Toronto? Toilet paper? No word fit.

"Gone, too?" October asked, amused somehow at Orson's troubles.

Orson tried to quickly rise from his cot, but still felt dizzy. His second approach was more cautious. "I'll find it," he insisted once he was successfully seated upright.

"I have no doubt you will," October assured him.

"Why—"

"Why are you losing information you knew only seconds ago?"

Orson nodded. He was slightly afraid that if he kept talking, he might lose some vital piece of information like his name or which bar on 7th street makes the best Negroni.

"The energy used to implant these memories into your cerebellum has a half-life. I would have undergone the

148

process myself, but sadly with my advanced years the process would have surely killed me. At least, I think it would. Even more tragic, the process will keep diminishing in effect for the rest of your life. I'm afraid you will never be quite as brilliant as you were about twenty minutes ago."

"I was asleep twenty minutes ago!"

"Like I said, *tragic*," October said. "But it isn't anywhere near as tragic as—"

"—as the nearly three hundred-fifty times Kan-ur has annihilated the people of Earth," Orson offered, taking it upon himself to be the one man in the room with the most information.

"That's right." October's face went suddenly dark. "What did you say?"

"I'll never be more brilliant than I was when I was asleep!"

"Before that."

"Three-hundred fif—" Orson gasped, realizing what he had just said. He rose from his cot.

October thumbed a nearby control mechanism. "Alert. The graft is cascading in on itself." October tried to hold Orson steady, but the younger man moved too erratically.

"Shut up!" Orson tried to make sense of the thoughts flooding into his head. "You were about to ask me if I know how to defeat Kan-ur, yes?"

October faltered, but did not remove his hand from Orson's shoulders. When Orson finally said, "I know how to do it," he turned back to his communication device.

"Stand down," October told those on the other end of the line. "You have my attention, young man."

"It's simple. The way to beat Kan-ur has been in plain sight this whole time. We have to stop trusting him."

# CHAPTER NINE

October's call to stand down fell on deaf ears, as a contingent of medics filed into Orson's recovery room. Goodman followed quickly behind. He held his hand over the pistol still locked in his hip holster. Orson didn't need the experience of hundreds of lifetimes to know Goodman fully intended to euthanize the patient if need be.

The medics flashed lights in Orson's eyes and proceeded to test other autonomic responses. He allowed this poking and prodding to proceed for a few seconds, but when his patience ebbed, it evaporated completely. He had no need of medical attention. The hundreds of voices in his head insisted he was perfectly sane. Orson pulled away from their ministrations and moved to a small computer unit next to the center where October had left his once trusty and now useless weapon.

Orson activated the machine and made fast work of bending the technological wonder to his will. He managed this all despite having never dreamed of such a device an hour earlier. S.B. flashed into and out of existence faster than most people could observe. Orson replaced the spectral electronic guide with a projection of a photograph.

Although taken in color, the image had significantly decreased in sharpness over both years and repeated copying.

Orson ceased his work with the machine long enough to once again swat away one of the medic's efforts to stabilize him. "Does anyone know what this photograph is?"

October and Goodman exchanged worried glances as the medics renewed their efforts.

"What is this photo?" Orson repeated.

"Every school child knows this photo." Goodman's tone softened, for once. The shift only agitated Orson further. As long as October's lackey remained thoroughly unimpressed with Orson, he hadn't become the subject of pity.

"What is it?" Orson asked once more. He hoped his insistence could urge Goodman back to his previous state of agitation.

Goodman pointed to the people in the photograph, huddled closely together in the terraformed Martian landscape. "Those people are our ancestors, foolishly hoping that their savior would come from the stars." He pointed to the nebulous, shadowy figure that lorded above them from a high balcony. "And that is Kan-ur, offering us that salvation at a price we couldn't possibly comprehend."

Orson snapped his fingers. "Wrong!" The medics stalled in their advance upon him, kept at bay only by the frown on October's face that appeared to be somewhere between intense worry and profound curiosity. The photograph metamorphosed before their eyes. "Mr. Goodman, you can see with your own eyes, but you do not understand. We are meant to think of your description as accurate. In many ways it is. However, that bastard has been lying to us for so long, we never even bothered to question the first lies he ever told us."

The photo now looked somewhat similar to its previous form, if only in relative composition. The mass of people still huddled upon the Martian landscape, but they didn't seem desperate. They didn't look as if total annihilation waited for them if they weren't delivered from their self-inflicted fate. They looked entitled, as if their dominion over the Earth of the past was a forgone conclusion.

Kan-ur had disappeared. In his place a thin, bearded man with an aristocratic bearing and aquiline features lorded over the Martian masses. Orson's memories of this man were dim, beyond the presence of a mysterious stone statue in his image from one of the more recent iterations.

"Who in the Hell is that?" Goodman asked.

The medics looked once again for their cues from October. Orson knew that he had already succeeded in convincing his older self that he wasn't crazy.

"Stand down," October repeated his order.

Orson relaxed his shoulder and once again considered the image. "That, Mr. Goodman, is Kan-ur."

The medics nearly resumed their attack on Orson regardless of October's objections. Orson's increasingly calm demeanor kept them at bay.

Goodman remained less than convinced of Orson's sanity. "That man can't be Kan-ur. He's *human*."

"So is Kan-ur," Orson countered. "Or, at least, some pieces of him were once a human being. Even I don't know what he is now."

Orson took their stunned silence as an invitation to continue.

"Don't you people know there are no such things as extra-terrestrials?"

\*     \*     \*

"You're just as bad as Kan-ur," Goodman insisted.

"I'm not saying that it isn't going to be difficult..." Orson countered.

They were in October's command center now. Orson hoped that the more advanced equipment would aid him as he made his point. He also suspected that the wide open space would make it more difficult to sedate him if the others continued to judge his ideas as insane.

"Perhaps we can try another transmission to the people of the Earth," Goodman attempted.

"Bah!" both Orson and October hissed at the same instant. They exchanged an uncomfortable glance before Orson continued. "Since we—I—the other fellow—first rebelled against that bastard, we've tried this same 'appeal to the masses' play several times. The people in this time are skeptical enough of Kan-ur, but that doesn't mean they'll trust us more. They don't trust anything. The same reality slowly imploding Kan-ur's new world means we'll never be able to stop him sooner. No. *No.* This is the only way."

"You want to destroy the arch?" Goodman asked.

"If for no other reason than it has never been tried before." Orson nodded, but only after he made the statement. For his certitude, he received a perfect vacuum of support, even from October. "We have to remember two things as we proceed—"

"*If* we proceed." Goodman and Orson stared each other down for a moment before the prior added, "Which we won't."

Orson ignored him. "First: you think Kan-ur has slaughtered billions of lives, when in reality he has to date obliterated *quadrillions* of lives and shows no sign of slowing down any time soon.

"Second: *Everything* he has ever said is a lie. We've spent lifetimes buying into the notion that our world is doomed without him, but loathing the way he goes about saving it. We don't need to be making these time jumps at all. Yes, we'll start to run out of breathable air, and vegetables will be the stuff of antiquated fantasy. But humanity will adapt. We've learned to build all of these technological nightmares we now run from, we might be able to put our collective creativity to use and save the human race without killing anyone."

"You'll never be able to get back to your own time," Goodman said. "I'm not saying that's a deal breaker for me, but I can't imagine you've thought all of this through to its natural conclusion."

Orson looked to October. They couldn't read each other's minds *per se*, but they were closer than any other two people to performing the feat. "The world will get along just fine without Orson Welles," the younger man said.

"Although this world will have to deal with two of us for the foreseeable future," October remarked. The notion amused him greatly.

"I renew my objections." Goodman offered up the remark to no one in particular; that was precisely the number of people still listening to him.

For the first time in any of Orson's myriad lifetimes, it seemed that there were only two possible iterations of what would happen next. First, their words would succeed in rousing Goodman from his immovable opposition to Orson's plan. Second, he would remain intractable, they would orbit round and round this issue past the time Kanur could use to destroy humanity seven or eight times.

As it turned out, they were wrong again. The

overflowing infinitude of possible outcomes for any situation in life—including the proper strategy for dethroning an ancient cyborg from the future—allowed for possibilities that none of them had considered.

In one possibility, a wisp of humanity still remaining in the stray bones and wires that made up Kan-ur came to the surface, and the supreme leader chose that moment to reach out to October's small band of insurgents on this asteroid to come to a peaceful, equitable solution to the ongoing conflict. Given that a nearly infinite series of similarly improbable possibilities existed, this one outlier required no further comment.

In another, Goodman in that instant tapped into a vein of inspiration and devised an entirely different plan to combat Kan-ur and his forces. Orson and October would be leery of the plan. Orson knew that a plan of attack similar to Goodman's suggestion was attempted in Iteration 344, and achieved the same results they were so desperate to avoid now. Unfortunately, the sheer weight of influence he had over these two men forced the three to try it. The results were tragically the same, and events moved forward towards Iteration 349 and one step closer to a reality that could not withstand another iteration.

There was yet a third unconsidered possibility that involved Orson succumbing right then to the mental stresses of his procedure and at that moment beginning to compulsively—in lieu of normal speech—make sounds identical to a koala bear during mating season. Orson would continue to act on this compulsion for the remainder of his living days, which thankfully numbered few. Kan-ur made quick work of the insurgents when they only had a disproportionately large, leaf-eating bear to lead them.

The most pertinent possible outcome of Goodman,

October and Orson's heated discussion was this: Just as Goodman was about to speak, moments before just a slight deficiency in adrenaline would bring about the birth of Orson the Koala, and long after the ghost of iterations past visited Kan-ur, his forces finally found the asteroid that was in fact not an asteroid, and opened fire.

*      *      *

They aimed their first volley squarely at the energy plant of the asteroid base. The hope on the part of the Earth army was that confusion among October's forces would make neutralization a quick prospect. They might have accomplished this by directly attacking the hangar deck. It currently held their meager fighter wing, and Goodman's ship, the *Oneida V*. It was their only means of escape. Instead, Kan-ur specifically instructed his gunner officer to lay down his fire in the pattern that they did. Far from having a change of heart about his eons-long reign of destruction, Kan-ur had an entirely different plan for October. He wanted to be free of Orson Welles—*all* Orsons Welles—meddling in his affairs once and for all. He too also wanted to enjoy the ultimate reveal of this final encounter.

*      *      *

For the three arguing back in the asteroid, the shudder of the attack had sent each of their stomachs sinking, as it became abundantly clear that there may not have been time for a thorough argument about their best course of action. They all moved as quickly as they could out of the area while it was still in mid-shudder.

Support beams above them groaned from external

pressure as Orson sprinted for the exit, October dawdled forward without his cane, and Goodman lagged behind in his attempt to keep October with them. All three stopped as a cave-in formed a sudden stalactite in the center. Metal scaffolding twisted and warped under the weight of the asteroid's imminent collapse.

Orson froze in place, but was sufficiently close to the exit as to avoid danger. Goodman leapt to push October out of the way of a now bent, jagged, and particularly menacing piece of falling scaffolding. Orson extended his hand to help Goodman up. They both crouched down once more to assist October. Goodman froze in his horror when confronted with the damage that had been done.

October seemed serene enough, aside from the trickle of light pink blood running from the side of his mouth. He coughed once so loud that it seemed to rattle the structure of the base further. The flow of blood only worsened. The large blade of warped metal that had only moments before been of such grave concern to Goodman now extended out of October's mid-section, wicking a second flow of dark red fluid onto the floor. Orson couldn't help but let his mind wander to a brief calculation of how many times he had stood over his own dying body, his feet in a puddle of his own blood. He also tried not dwelling on his diminishing memories of being on the other side of this scenario.

October tried to rise, increasing the outflow of carnage. Goodman cried out in a vain attempt to get him to stop his climb, but Orson said nothing. Nothing more could be done.

"Go," October rasped. With his last electron of physical strength he gingerly—his drifting consciousness would allow nothing stronger than that—grabbed Goodman's arm.

"I'm sorry I couldn't do more," October insisted.

He found it impossible to pull himself from October's side. It was only after a second, improbably loud and clear "Go!" from October that he sprinted from the hangar and left both October and Orson behind.

Orson approached the old, mortally wounded man slowly. They needed not to exchange any words.

He knew that strained, although ultimately terrified look on October's face all too well. He grabbed the spindly arm of metal sticking out of October's body and prepared to thrust upward, completing the job that the scaffolding had only the nerve to begin, but not the courage to finish.

But then Orson stopped. Despite the continued look of understanding between the two men born of one identity, Orson couldn't bring himself to suicide, even if it was only after a fashion.

"What?" October asked. Orson knew the old man thought he would be dead by now.

"What if this works and everything is put back the way it was supposed to be? Isn't it possible that whatever is waiting for humanity on Earth is far worse?"

The answer came to Orson the instant he finished asking the question. In the charred remains of that cursed sword, there were implications of enough indigenous demons able to destroy the planet under their own power. Orson supposed that whatever lay ahead for humanity, the potential horrors it could inflict upon itself were finite, whereas the hell it now endured knew no end.

October found some degree of motion and swatted away Orson's hand from the metal bar. His eyes bore down into his younger self. "Don't waste another moment with me! Go!" he rasped after flinging Orson's hand away.

Orson left himself behind. The memory of what it felt like to die in that moment echoed through his mind as he fled.

For his part, October waited for Kan-ur's ground troops to begin their inevitable invasion. If any of the troopers were unlucky enough to find October, they would be in for the verbal abuse of their lives.

They never found him.

# CHAPTER TEN

Orson ran to catch up with Goodman and was relieved to gain on him just as he boarded his ship. The chase was complicated by the electrical discharges of a firefight between ground troops.

Goodman jumped into the lead pilot seat and began the craft's power-up routine. "If you're coming with me, then take a seat, but we're going to do this my way."

Orson acquiesced. Scant hours earlier, the smooth surfaces of the craft's cabin had been as alien to him as a trip beyond the planet Mars. Now the craft and its myriad predecessors were like a second home to him. He even designed some of the more improvised upgrades. Still, Orson wasn't a natural pilot like Rebecca.

Orson shook his head. Goodman was the pilot. Who the hell was Rebecca?

If Orson were to have any hope of cutting through his rage and grief and engage in his own plan, he would have one shot at re-routing control of the craft to the secondary pilot's station where Goodman had ordered him to sit. The only obstacle that stood between Orson and success was a small lever above the controls in front of him. He just had to move his hand a little bit farther—

"That will be far enough," a voice called out to Orson. He instantly recoiled, assuming he would have to take another tactic in his effort to destroy the arch. The voice was tinny, as if it weren't coming from within the *Oneida* and was instead broadcast from a distant radio.

Orson turned around in his seat to see Kan-ur standing at the rear of the ship. He immediately stepped away from the auxiliary control. Goodman rose from his seat as well, staring with only marginally contained fury at the intruder.

"Where's the old man?" Kan-ur asked. He breezily swayed his pistol back and forth between Orson and Goodman.

"That's rich, coming from the oldest man in recorded history," Orson sneered. Up until that moment, he knew, but couldn't quite feel his level of disgust with the black clad figure in front of him. Now, even with lifetimes of memories escaping his consciousness every second, Orson's contempt for the thing that was once a man was palpable.

"Droll, young Mr. Welles. I don't believe we've been properly introduced."

"Oh, we've met, sir. *Hundreds* of times."

There was doubt in Kan-ur for the first time in ages, and it only started with Orson's uncharacteristic ease with the current situation.

"October's dead," Goodman offered, the second word of the revelation warbled as it left his throat.

The orb of Kan-ur's head shifted on its axis. Whatever was left of those shrewd, piercing eyes from the picture Orson had uncovered now looked squarely at Goodman.

"Pity," Kan-ur cooed. "I always enjoy the opportunity to end his life on these little trips of mine." His head shifted again to re-consider Orson. "Although I suppose watching you bleed out will be a sufficient consolation prize."

Kan-ur moved slowly towards Orson, like an animal in prelude to an attack. In doing so, he managed to neglect what should have been the true source of his worries. Goodman attacked first, tackling Kan-ur to the ground with surprising ease.

Orson thought quickly. He determined that their physical altercation had little if nothing to do with him. He never enjoyed admitting that something—anything—was not about him. He whipped back around to the controls he had previously hoped no one was aware he knew how to operate. He transferred control to his own console. The panels in front of him lit up.

While the other two continued their tussle, Orson carefully programmed his desired course into the craft's computer as accurately as he could. His ineptitude behind the yoke of any vehicle—coupled with his only light and breezy familiarity with structural engineering of extra-atmospheric mega structures—led to his effort being not terribly more reliable than a child's flailing guess. Orson activated the craft's engines.

Kan-ur and Goodman might have taken the opportunity of their unexpected lift off to panic, but they were far too engrossed in their mutual efforts to cut off the other's air supply to notice they were now in flight. Kan-ur offered a swift hit to Goodman's trachea. The pilot smacked down to the deck, rasping to regain his breath.

Kan-ur moved on from his victory and marched over to the pilot's seat. With undiminished swiftness, he wrapped his arm around the secondary pilot's seat. It extended beyond his reach. Kan-ur extended his arms beyond their normal length in a flash. Orson could see the appendages begin to move around to restrain him, and was able to slide out of the chair before they tightened.

Kan-ur's arms slid back to their former length as he towered over Orson. With almost no success, Orson attempted to tackle Kan-ur at the legs. The struggle began with Kan-ur at more of an advantage than he had with Goodman. Orson's fast moves only served him for a moment. Kan-ur pulled him to his feet, a position from which there was no escape. Kan-ur only offered Orson relief by way of letting him move away from the wall, only to push him straight to the ground.

"You are trying to destroy everything w—*I* worked for," Kan-ur warbled. Orson could have sworn the orb where Kan-ur's head should have been began to glow red with his fury.

Beyond the craft's windows, the flashes of the battle raged on. The bright metallic curve of the Martian arch filled the porthole windows more than any volley from opposing ships.

"What have you done?" Goodman wheezed as he made his way to the main piloting controls. That he directed the question at Orson was the only thing that could have distracted Kan-ur in his zeal to wring the life out of Orson.

Kan-ur released him and made his way to the control panel. He knocked Goodman back towards the bulkhead and took in the information for himself. His head rotated back to once again look at Orson.

"Never let it be said that you two can't agree on anything," Orson said.

"You set us on a direct course for the base of the arch. You intend to destroy it," Kan-ur whispered.

"*And* I locked our course in. I'm a much better pilot than either of you thought. Wait. That doesn't help my case with either of you," Orson added much more softly.

"Forget I said that—"

Kan-ur zipped back from the pilot's station and quickly wrapped his upper extremities around Orson's neck again. Orson happened upon two truths in that moment. First, breathing was sufficiently difficult that he wondered if the ship were already crashing into its intended target. Second, the crimson tinge to Kan-ur's orb-head was now either a sign that Orson was quickly losing consciousness or that Kan-ur's intense emotions were actually visually manifesting themselves in his equipment. The visceral heat Orson felt pointed to the latter.

"You have *murdered* all of humanity," Kan-ur hissed.

Orson wanted to tell Kan-ur how he could only hope to be a competent amateur in the shadow of Kan-ur's genius. He also wanted to laugh in what was still left of the bastard's face. Mostly, he wanted to catch his breath. Failing that he would settle for finally relenting to the sleep that so desperately wanted to claim him.

Ultimately, he just couldn't keep his mouth shut. "Humanity will be fine," Orson spat, the sudden restful comfort he found in this improbable position crashed down on him like a wave. "Without either of—"

Orson didn't get to finish his final statement in defiance of Kan-ur, for death suddenly filled the ship. The heat spiked around Orson as Kan-ur's head cracked open. Viscera exploded forth, and Kan-ur's body slumped to the ground. Orson could finally breathe, but every hungry gulp of air was tinged with copper and some other ingredient he couldn't quite place. Orson slumped to the ground as well. In the charred, cracked, and yet still somehow wet remains of Kan-ur's skull, Orson could swear he saw the remains of an eyeball among the frayed wires and machinery. The organ belonged to a man who was even now becoming an increasingly hazy memory.

Orson looked off from the perfected synthesis of human carnage and over-heated computer that was Kan-ur. Goodman still held his side-arm outward. Orson rose from his splayed position on the deck, although he did so slowly. He couldn't be perfectly certain that such a conclusive injury would actually kill what was left of his enemy, not after Kan-ur had unnaturally extended his life for so long.

Once Orson could be sure—just as Kan-ur's appendages ceased their final convulsions—that the man was dead, he stepped towards Goodman. "I was just about to let loose with a particularly choice array of words that would have brought his delicate ego down in flames."

Goodman arced his neck to look at Kan-ur's remains. "Yeah." He turned back to Orson. "That would have worked, too."

Orson braced himself to argue the point, but a violent shudder within the craft stalled the discussion as the two turned their attention away from one another and towards the craft's controls. By now, the massive base of the Martian Arch filled all three cockpit windows and beyond.

For a moment, Goodman considered attempting to alter their course and put the kibosh on Orson's plan. But, when he realized their relative distance from the arch and the grim data from the battle near their asteroid base, reality refused to give way to his desire not to give up the fight. Kan-ur was finally dead, but he had grown beyond the small frame that lay on the deck. He was a force of nature. His followers were legion. In a few short moments, that would not be Goodman's problem anymore.

"I hope you're right," Goodman finally said. Once again, Orson was about to offer an indignant retort, but the *Oneida* interrupted him by hitting its target.

*   *   *

As the Martian Arch collapsed in on itself in a torrent of brilliant light, it was clear to the survivors of both Kan-ur and October's armies that things would never be the same.

Time and resources to rebuild the arch had long since run out when the authorities examined the wreckage. It took decades to build the arch with Kan-ur's close supervision, and the earth only had six months' worth of resources to support itself at the current rate of consumption.

But, as it turned out, Orson had been right all along. Humanity *would* be just fine without Kan-ur and Orson Welles both. Difficult days followed for the humans of Earth, to be sure, but with judicious use of the resources they had left on both Earth and Mars, humanity was able to thrive once more. After several decades of toil and strife, they were even able to—slowly—rehabilitate those locked into terrible lives outside the habitable zones.

Eventually, humanity came to grips with their numbed complicity in the horrors that befell the twelve-score multiverse and forged their own future. The names of both Kan-ur and October slipped into half-remembered legend.

*       *       *

THURSDAY, JULY 12TH, 1984
1:45 PM COORDINATED MARTIAN TIME
ITERATION...
ITERATION...
ITERATION...
JUST BEYOND MARTIAN ORBIT
*THE ONEIDA V*

Orson awoke with a start. He was mildly surprised to still be alive. This assumed he truly was alive, and this wasn't the entrance to the afterlife, but that hardly accounted for the jerked motion upward his reflexes forced upon him. As awareness returned, he mainly focused on his desire to not be lying in Kan-ur's remains.

As he looked around the cabin, the bay windows were filled with streaks of light. He turned and saw Goodman had already awoken from his unconsciousness—if he had even suffered any—and was back at his pilot's seat.

"Where are we?" Orson asked.

"No idea," Goodman said. "Before you ask, 'When?' I'm getting the sinking feeling that the arch was still active as it collapsed in on itself."

Goodman tried to sound sure of his assessment, but as he had offered no actual information, he failed.

"You mean...?" Orson asked.

\* \* \*

SUNDAY, AUGUST 12, 1951
ITERAT—

"Yes. I mean. We're heading back towards 1938. Unfortunately, we're moving at such a high velocity that the relativity readings are all over the place. We could be in the Middle Ages for all I know."

"Well, here's hoping..." If they were truly unstuck in time with no escape, Orson actually pulled for Elizabethan England. He figured he could do quite well then, despite the competition.

"If we are in any sort of time frame appropriate for you," Goodman continued through gritted teeth. He struggled to keep ahold of the manual controls. "There's no guarantee I'll be able to nose this damned thing towards Earth with any reliability. We're just as likely to shoot through Mercury's polar caps right before we burst into flames."

"Very well. You can stop trying to make me feel better."

"I wasn't," Goodman grunted as the controls offered another shimmy. "Even if we are in the right time and even if we are in the right place, there's almost no chance we'll crash land on any part of Earth that won't kill us on sight."

\*     \*     \*

FRIDAY, SEPTEMBER 5, 1941
ITERATION UNKNOWN

"It would beat the time we crashed an escape pod in the middle of a Kansas farm field and only had a tractor and three head of cattle to help us raise an army."

"That didn't happen." Goodman nearly relinquished his pressure on the controls in the middle of his confusion.

"Y—" Orson began, but then stopped. He may have been relieved that Earth, bright and alive, was squarely in the center cockpit window and the flames of their re-entry into the atmosphere should soon follow. It may have also been that another phantom memory crossed his mind and dissipated the moment it was accessed. "I'm not really sure."

It was only then that Orson nursed the growing fear that the memories implanted by October's sword—and for that matter, any memories he may have possessed prior to the procedure—would evaporate the instant he dwelled upon them. He wondered how it would feel to be completely dispossessed of any trace element of what it meant to be Orson Welles. Would it be a calamity that would enfeeble him for the rest of his days? Would it be freeing?

"There's another ship locked in the distortion with us!" Goodman cried as he quickly glanced at the alarm on his board.

"One of Kan-ur's—"

"I have no idea. I'm a little busy at the moment."

"What do we do?" Orson asked.

"Our fates are the same," Goodman said grimly.

"Stop trying to make me feel better!" As the ship did not appear to slow down, Orson knew the next few seconds would hurt. The anticipation was overwhelming.

\*    \*    \*

SATURDAY, OCTOBER 29TH, 1938
6:45 AM EST
ITERATION ZERO
GROVER'S MILL, NEW JERSEY
EARTH

What is a barn if no farming took place there? The town of Grover's Mill had all but shut down under the weight of the Great Depression. For months after the economy threatened to dismantle them, the people of the town thought that things would get better, but eventually reality had to set in. Somewhere westward those migrant farmers wondered about what would come to the small Jersey town first, relief and booming production, or the decay of the barns that used to house their bounty.

None of them thought that the first thing to hit Grover's Mill in years would be a flying saucer the size of a small yacht.

Orson did not have the luxury of being knocked unconscious by the second crash of the *Oneida* in as many minutes. The impact strengthened the dull ache that replaced Orson's head. It confirmed through one of the least pleasant manners possible that he was still alive.

Goodman's headache had disappeared, apparently. Orson found his reluctant co-pilot thrown clear of his chair. The blank expression on Goodman's face and the wet gash on the left side of his neck told Orson all he needed to know. Whatever awaited Orson outside of the ship, he would have to face it alone.

Despite the faint glow of the ship's inner workings still in operation, Orson had to physically force the main hatch open. Blue sky blinded him, but the sight of it was an encouraging sign. The north pole of Mercury would have to wait. He was in some semi-civilized portion of the planet, but that left plenty of places that came complete with their own set of bad news.

More good news followed when the ship spit him out into the middle of a neglected, but otherwise idyllic farm. The remains of a barn littered the space beyond the ship. A billow of smoke cascaded from the field beyond. He jogged to the wreck of the other craft, but was heartened that the ship was in far worse condition than the *Oneida V*. Large sections of the hull spread out over the field.

Orson approached the wreckage of the other ship more closely. He used the sleeve of his tunic to wipe off a streak of mud covering the ships name and then nearly fainted. On the hull of the other ship, beneath its cocoon of mud lay the words "Oneida II."

Orson looked behind him just in time to see a weapon he hadn't seen in ages aimed at his head. It was the only development since he emerged that didn't shock him beyond belief.

The woman holding the weapon looked older than Orson's more profound memories allowed. Streaks of gray in her hair and a patch covering the left eye made her seem older, but this was Rebecca. No one before had the opportunity to meet their oldest friend for the first time.

"It's you," they both said in the same instant.

"But you're young..." Rebecca remarked.

"And you're..." Orson immediately thought better of the counterpoint. "Holding up nicely. Well done."

"How did this happ—?"

Rebecca's question died a quick death as Orson hopped away and squealed. "It's like I've never been one step ahead of any of you people before! I may be the smartest man in all of the Solar System! That's extraordinary! When we destroyed the arch, it sent a dangerously unstable version of the tunnel outward in every direction of the space-time continuum! That's why we've had those electrical distortions between Earth and Mars over the years! It was me, or rather, us traveling backward through the ages one last time! That's what took your ship in Iteration 344! You didn't die!"

Rebecca attempted to interrupt him. It was a lost cause before she began.

"Not now, Rebecca! I don't have time to explain every little detail for those of you just entering the story!"

"You destroyed the arch?" she persisted.

Orson jumped again and offered a kick to an imaginary foe. "That's the best part! It's all over! That fellow with the fishbowl bulb for a head thought he could vanquish me, but he forgot one crucial thing about Orson Welles!" He moved quickly back to Rebecca, wanting to make sure he didn't lose her again. To punctuate his point, he slapped his forehead with enough force to dislodge a previously vivid memory of washing up on the coast of Oahu. "There are hundreds of us!"

\* \* \*

"Is that—?"

Orson looked at Kan-ur's remains, but still did not want to get too close. "Yes. Like I said: It's all over."

Rebecca pointed to Goodman's body. "And that?"

"A friend," Orson said. "Well, not a friend, precisely. He loathed me, truth be told, but he wasn't actively trying to kill me."

"That is what passes for a friend in your world," Rebecca remarked as she approached the instruments of the new craft. She was able to work the machinery of the *Oneida V* fairly well, despite the advancements that had been made in the intervening years. After a few moments of contemplation, she rose again from her seat. "Stop right there. You flew this ship through the arch?"

"Uhh..." Orson knew he had run afoul somewhere, but he couldn't quite narrow it down. "Yes?"

"What is my one rule?" she spat.

He realized his error, but was once again trapped. "I don't fly—"

"You don't fly things. That's right. If I ever see you fly another ship again, I'll be the one to kill you."

Orson put his hands up in submission, and yet his smile muddled the message. "Yes ma'am." His true friends often wanted very much to kill him.

Rebecca returned to her instruments while Orson walked around the cabin to see if any of the remaining equipment would be of any use.

"It's 1938!"

Orson briefly lamented not spending the rest of his days in the era of Shakespeare. "Like I never left... See? I can fly with the best of them."

Rebecca glared at Orson. He opted not to press the point further.

"I won't presume to speak for you, Rebecca... But I could certainly grow accustomed to saving the world on a regular basis. I can get out of the theater racket—"

"We're in New Jersey!" Rebecca reported.

"Ha! We can walk home from here!"

"Orson..." Rebecca reproached.

"We won't. We travelled fifty years and 250,000 miles. We're not about to walk through the Lincoln Tunnel. Where was I? Ah, yes! Saving the world as a new vocation. Maybe I won't have to give up the theater. I can do both part-time. Although, I might have to wear that damn cape or some other nonsense. I hadn't considered that—"

"Orson!" Rebecca called out again. "Watch this!"

Orson moved to Rebecca's location. The display showed a view from low Martian orbit. Orson hoped it was the last time he would ever look at the particular vista. Where previous iterations had built their arch, clear cosmos hung in perfect suspension. Phobos—the moon that housed their base in the early days of the resistance—hung in the distance.

"Hell of a time to feel nostalgic for the good old days, my friend," Orson said.

Rebecca shook her head. "This was a recording the ship made ten minutes ago, just after this ship emerged from the distortion near Earth." She manipulated the controls further. Slowly but surely, another rift formed in the gate's place.

"Is that—?" Orson asked.

"Yes. They somehow managed to re-activate the arch. Everything you did was for nothing. Here we go again."

Orson sighed and sunk down into the other control

chair. Visions of the sky on fire with an emerald hue floated through his mind, and they did not dissipate. In his despair, something struck Orson. He had seen the arch's rift open countless times before, but he had only vague memories of this particular distortion's shape and color. It was almost as if...

He looked at Kan-ur's body. "I don't know about reactivated, Rebecca. But you're right. This is far from over."

The power in the ship gave out at that moment, leaving Orson and Rebecca in total darkness.

# INTERLUDE

Humanity had long since stopped looking at the now-dim orb in the Martian sky that had once been their home. The events that sent them looking for a new home in the bosom of the God of War were so long ago that they didn't seem important anymore.

The Scientist was different. He couldn't help but look at that dot in the sky. The insistence of humanity to ignore the Earth, even going so far as to look past their culpability in its poisoning, infuriated him. Gleeful ignorance of history was humanity's greatest ongoing folly.

Trying to restore that dot in the sky became an obsession with the Scientist. The rapid, if haphazard, terraforming of Mars meant that surely they could one day restore the Earth to its former glory. Alas, after making the restoration of the Earth his all-consuming goal for nearly all of his adult life, the Scientist came to the crushing revelation that the poison filling the Terran atmosphere had no need or capacity for mercy, not unlike their creators. The poison clouds were strong, adaptive, and showed no sign of dissipating. Some other idea would be necessary.

The idea finally came. If a habitable Earth was a thing of the past, then all of their efforts should be committed to arriving at that destination. The idea was impractical, if not preposterous. No one at the Olympus Institute—before subsequent developments made him chairman—paid any attention to time travel and its practical applications. The power needed for such a plan to become feasible did not occur in nature. Providence provided a development that suddenly transformed the Scientist from a well-meaning crank into a prescient voice from the future.

After colonizing the fourth planet in their solar system, humanity became abundantly aware that beneath the surface of the red planet were not the insectoid murderers of H.G. Wells, or the noble savages of Edgar Rice Burroughs, but unimaginable quantities of energy. The energy could run all of humanity's new Martian cities for years, if it didn't immediately set fire to those cities in the process. The power was far too volatile to operate anything with internal circuitry more complicated than a toaster oven.

The electricity beneath the red planet's rocky surface could also power something much larger than the cities, so long as the machinery involved was relatively simple.

It took years to construct the arch that would deliver mankind from disaster. It took ruthlessness in the guise of actions the man never thought he would be able to live with under previous circumstances. It took this man to the very boundaries of his humanity.

But there he stood in the observation atrium of

Olympus Mons University beholding his magnificent arch.

A call came through, interrupting his reverie. He clicked the phone's control and said nothing, allowing the caller to speak.

"Sir, we just received word from the doctor." The man's underling took long enough to fill the silence. The news couldn't be good. Normally the Scientist relished hearing from his right-hand man. The underling served as Chief Aide to the three most recent chairpeople of the Institute, and the knowledge that he would never advance further in his career was among the several predictions that re-enforced his reputation as a clairvoyant.

"And?" the Scientist asked. He already knew the information before the call had come in. He could feel it in his bones. If the conversation were to be at all productive, then he knew he had to show a passing interest in the matters that others regarded with grave importance.

"Without another surgery you will have another few weeks at most. Even then there are no guarantees with the experimental nature of the procedure."

He didn't need weeks. When his work was done, he could freely die.

"Very well," he finally remarked with enough dispassion so as to put a close to the topic. "Status of the arch?"

Again there was silence on the other end of the connection as the Chief Aide considered pressing the issue of surgery. Further discussion would prove fruitless.

"The arch is ready, sir."

For the first time in decades, the man felt a surge of what could only be natural endorphins. His heart had long since aged past the point where it could handle the manufactured stimulants that fueled their new Martian society. This could also be the sensation one felt before death. If this was the end, he knew that things would proceed without him.

Shooting pains radiated through his arm. It became apparent the momentum of events would be his only deliverance.

"Make sure..." he trailed off. Just as a profound, unexpressed truth floated through his mind, there was no more.

\*     \*     \*

The Chief Aide sounded the alert the instant it became clear his superior was having trouble. He and the medics forced entry into the observation deck. It was far too late. If the corpse née Chairman née Scientist had been wheeled into surgery during that phone call instead of being told he needed the surgery, there might have been a chance for his survival. Now, he would go down in history as expiring mere moments before realizing his life's great work.

The Lead Medic sealed the body containment unit and sent his people to their work. The Chairman's remains would be handled much like anyone else's in the New Martian Society. With just an ounce of thrust, the body containment unit would be sent on its final course. Unless it drifted off into the great expanse of the cosmos it would meet with the poisoned orb from which they came. This almost never happened, despite the popular paranoia that modern funereal science was a fiendishly simple scam and such wanderings happened all the time.

On approach to the Earth, the body would not burn up in the planet's atmosphere. The pressure of the dense remaining air would crush the container and then, ultimately, his flesh. The Chairman would finally return to the planet of his ancestors, as was always his plan.

"Is there anything further you need from us, Chairman?" the Lead Medic asked. The Chief Aide had spent his life in quiet servitude to the leaders of the Olympus Institute. Now, he was that leader.

The former underling just then realized that the operation of the great machine above them and the fate of the people who were to travel through it were now entirely in his hands.

"No," the new Chairman replied. "He did a miraculous job of setting things in motion.

"On second thought, once we've made our way through the arch, I will need a full medical workup."

"Of course, sir. We will spare no effort to keep you alive and healthy."

"Thank you."

"Thank *you*, Chairman Kan-ur," the lead medic said earnestly. "We're all counting on you."

The lead medic left Kan-ur alone. He looked up to the arch that had so thoroughly dominated his life and the lives of so many others. He wondered what this turn might mean for him and the course of his life. He couldn't possibly fathom all of the possible consequences, but to see the future was not his task. His only job was to put the past to some use.

# CHAPTER ELEVEN

SATURDAY, OCTOBER 29, 1938
10:30 AM EST
ITERATION ZERO
MERCURY THEATRE OFFICES
MANHATTAN, NY
EARTH

"He's been *gone* for nearly a week, Roger!" John Houseman screamed into the phone. "No one's even heard from him since Wednesday!"

"It was your idea to send him out here, John," Roger Hill said calmly, infuriatingly so with the blatant rebuke woven into the soothing tone.

"I know that!" A knock came at Houseman's office door. "Come in!" he barked.

The office secretary, Joanna, shuffled in. She had an insistent expression on her face.

"I swear to God, Roger. If you are hiding that boy from me, if you are both trying to teach me some ill-conceived lesson, I will *ruin* the both of you."

"If Orson doesn't reappear soon, John, I imagine you'd

be the only one courting ruin," Hill explained.

"Go to Hell," Houseman spat back as he slammed the phone receiver on its hook. His head snapped towards Joanna. "What?!" His anger didn't know where to go; it was looking for Orson.

"I think I've found him," she explained.

"At the bottom of a lake, no doubt," Houseman guessed. Never before and never again would he feel such a perfect blend of simultaneous joy and dread at the possibility of Orson Welles being alive and well.

Joanna shook her head. "New Jersey."

"He would have done better for himself in the lake," Houseman went to grab his coat. It was times like these he wished he owned a gun.

*     *     *

"I don't see that as an unreasonable request!" Orson cried out from across the table. Rebecca sat beside him and had said nothing since they wandered onto the Princeton Campus. Their appearance, coupled with Orson's extensive statements about invaders from the future, greatly alarmed the University's population and said more than enough for the both of them.

The Detective that had been Orson and Rebecca's guide through the New Jersey criminal justice system took off his eyeglasses and rubbed the bridge of his nose.

"Mr. Welles, if that is your real name—I for one don't think you sound like the fella on the radio, but that's beside the point," the Detective said, "we are not going to allow you to lead us to an abandoned farm in Grover's Mill so that you can prove the veracity of your claims." The noise of a quick klaxon filled the interrogation room. The Detective answered the call from the telephone on the wall.

"We'd be pretty lousy at police work if we took a deal like that. Goodman here."

Orson's eyes went wide. He looked to Rebecca in an attempt to share the revelation of the coincidence, but the communication went nowhere.

Detective Goodman spoke to whoever was on the other end of the connection and immediately relaxed his posture. He hung up the phone. "You've made bail."

Orson rose to offer further protest, but the Detective cut him off. "You're free to go, and now, so am I."

The door leading out to the rest of the sheriff's office clanked open, revealing Houseman and his now possibly permanent scowl.

Orson nearly moved to grab the Detective by the shoulders, but stopped himself with a lurch. "No, you can't leave me with him. Anybody but *him*."

Houseman said nothing to Orson. Instead, he turned to the Detective. "Officer, may I have a few words with the prisoner before we leave and I murder him with great relish."

"Well, I'll give this much to you, fella," The Detective said as he took what he hoped was his last look at the man who claimed to be Orson Welles. "You must know him pretty well. You can have 10 minutes here, but if you're still here then I'm citing all of you for trespassing."

"What are you going to do then?" Orson asked. "Arrest us?"

The Detective had already left.

"Sit down," Houseman's tone was filled with rage, and yet barely audible.

Orson cooperated, but haughtily enough that it almost appeared impatient, as if his next barb towards the Detective would have been the difference between life and death. "First, and before I take my bail money back and leave you here for the rest of your life: Where have you been?"

"Mars," Orson replied.

Houseman's eyes went wide.

"No, the future," Orson corrected.

Houseman rose from his chair.

"No, wait. Mars," Orson tried. "Which one do you want to hear?"

Houseman turned back from the door. "I want the truth. I want to know why you're in a police station in New Jersey cavorting with some strange woman who is refreshingly older than you." Houseman looked at Rebecca. "Sorry. Also, is that blood on your shirt?"

"I assure you, most of the blood is mine," Orson said.

"What?"

"He's kidding," Rebecca interjected.

"She speaks!" Orson exclaimed. "Where were you when the Keystone Kops had us surrounded?"

She shrugged and said nothing further.

"Never mind," Orson said to Houseman, and gestured at the chair once occupied by the Detective. Slowly, Houseman took the indicated seat.

Orson told the story in full. Houseman gave no indication that he believed a word of it, but he hadn't left. It was progress.

"And what precisely do you want me to do about this...story of yours?" Houseman finally asked.

"You need to help me convince these police officers that they need to warn the military about the coming invasion," Orson said as if it were the simplest request in the world. His tone might have been an unforeseen side effect of the sword procedure, but he neglected to mention that part of the story to Houseman. Somehow, it seemed a bridge too far.

Houseman considered Orson's response for a moment—that, or his brain was becoming an object of pure rage-based frustration—before turning to Rebecca.

"So, I'm to understand you're a Martian?" Houseman asked Rebecca.

"Not exactly," she said, hesitating with both words. "But I haven't been born yet, if that makes any differ—"

"I trust you can find your way on your own," Houseman said to Orson as he again headed for the door.

"Housey..." Orson pleaded with the older man. He changed tones when it became clear that Housey meant to make good on his threats. "I think you're the one who will have a hard time finding his way on his own."

Houseman stopped at the door, but said nothing further.

"Have you always been such an insufferable bastard at this point in your life?" Rebecca asked Orson *sotto voce*. "Also, who the Hell is this guy?"

Orson shrugged in response to both questions. He then laughed as Houseman slammed his hand on the door. "I had a career before you. Sir—no matter what every single soul in all of creation thinks—I will be able to find work aside from being the personal whipping boy to the Great Boy Genius. I'll start right now. I'll produce the Hallowe'en show for *your* radio program despite the only help I get from you is this pulped H.G. Wells novella. I will have you know—"

"Wait," Orson said. It wasn't another plea. It was far softer than what Orson begging might have sounded like. In a flash, Orson was up from his seat and sprang for Houseman, grabbing his arms.

"What did you say?" he asked Houseman sharply.

Houseman entertained him, but only just so. "I—like everyone else—" he repeated, "will be just fine witho—"

"No, no," Orson insisted. "*After* that." He then looked at Rebecca. "After?"

She shrugged again.

"Before and after are sort of arbitrary concepts for me at the moment," Orson explained to Houseman. "Repeat the *other* thing."

"The matter of the impending Hallowe'en show? Or your plagiarizing of H.G. Wells in your attempts to find an alibi?"

Houseman got no auditory response from his charge. Orson slapped his hand against the door and howled in delight. "You're a genius, Housey! Don't let anyone tell you differently."

"What?" Rebecca asked.

"The old man had the right idea more often than he didn't," Orson said. It was as if Houseman were no longer in the room.

"What 'old man'?" Houseman asked.

"Myself," Orson hissed his reply, somewhere in the middle of several different epiphanies. "Christ, Housey. I don't have time to spit out exposition for people just now rejoining the story. Honestly, try to keep up."

He turned back to Rebecca. "He was always trying to win this thing with that damn broadcast to every corner of human civilization." She still wasn't following him, so Orson continued. "He was always trying to get the word out, as if when the people were confronted with the truth they would have no choice but to rise up and tear down the system."

"I'm now more lost than him. That plan never worked," Rebecca said.

"No. Of course it didn't!" Orson rattled quickly. "Quiet! I'm figuring things out! In the future, everyone's so cynical they would think you have an agenda if you were trying to untie them from a set of train tracks."

He moved to the solitary window in the room. Orson could almost see past the bars on the window to the quickly growing calamity in the Martian skies.

"Now, however, things are much different. With the Four Horsemen of the Apocalypse comprising the goodly chunk of the heads of state in Europe, and as people *expect* disaster...

"Why... they'd believe you even if the sky *weren't* falling!" Before, he was merely feeling the epiphany that brought him to his feet. Now he searched for the words to bring his two unlikely compatriots on board to his scheme.

"What are you trying to tell us?" Rebecca asked. Orson had already swung open the interrogation room door; he implicitly expected Rebecca and Houseman to follow him, despite their recent collective protests to the contrary.

Orson reached into his pocket and retrieved his pipe. He was fresh out of tobacco and several lifetimes away from his last match. It was no matter. Despite his scowling, Houseman would supply what he needed in due time.

Orson placed the pipe in his mouth. "We have a radio show to do."

# CHAPTER TWELVE

SATURDAY, OCTOBER 29TH, 1938
2:15 PM EST
ITERATION ZERO
CBS RADIO BUILDING
MANHATTAN, NY
EARTH

Just as the Mercury Theatre on the Air and their rehearsal director, Paul Stewart, finally worked out where "The Story of the Door" would fit into their Hallowe'en production of *The Strange Case of Dr. Jekyll and Mr. Hyde*, the studio fell into a wave of unproductive sentiment. The studio fell upon its own story of the door as the studio's main entryway swung open and their prodigal founder entered with enough fury and enough new female companionship that there was no other possibility other than the conclusion that Orson Welles had already been drinking.

"What are we doing?" Orson asked in the middle of his fitful entrance. He leveled all of his attention on their announcer, Dan Seymour. "What?!" he asked again.

Seymour shrank back from the encounter. It was far too early for him to be fighting with Orson.

"They're preparing *Jekyll and Hyde*, Orson. The show you instructed me to produce," Houseman explained.

"Bah!" Orson spat as he grabbed the script out of Stewart's hand. He gave the document a cursory glance—which Orson deemed to be an exceedingly polite gesture—before throwing it to the other end of the room. He then grabbed everyone else's scripts and disposed of them in a similar manner. Most members of the production were glad to give up their copy. If that was all Orson wanted, there wasn't anything to gain in resisting him further.

"Where's the damn writer?" Orson howled.

Howard Koch emerged from the gaggle, sadly eyeing the pile of rejected scripts.

"Yes, you!" Orson cried as he grabbed Koch by the lapel of his shirt. "You wrote a script for *War of the Worlds* before some mental deficient foolishly put you onto this Robert Louis Stevenson shit?"

"You would be the mental deficient," Houseman remarked. "*You* are the one who scuttled *War of the Worlds*."

"Quiet!" Orson barked back then turned his attention once more towards to Koch. "You also wrote *War of the Worlds*?"

Koch nodded.

"Do you still have that script?" Koch nodded again, more frantically this time. Koch reached for his worn, brown leather satchel. Orson grabbed the bag from Koch's hands to the collective horrified moans of his fellow performers. After a moment of rifling through the bag, he found the offending scenario. He spent a flash of a moment scanning the first several pages. As whatever information he was able to take in from the material seeped into whatever room Orson had left in his brain, he began to chuckle, offering the same aimless, guttural noise normally reserved for Dwight Frye.

"Do you like it?" Koch asked. The writer immediately gritted his teeth.

"It's not really my genre," Orson responded, punctuating the dismissal with a spiteful laugh.

"Is that a yes?"

"Of course I don't like it! What the hell do you think 'It's not really my genre' means?"

He snapped the script shut and tucked it under his arm. "But we are going to fix it, you and I," Orson told Koch, and then cried out to the studio, "Schmoogle Boogle!"

"That's enough," Houseman warned.

"Orson..." Rebecca gently attempted to remind Orson where and when he was.

Orson snapped his head between the two as he realized his error. "Typewriters!" Orson cried. "I meant to say I need a typewriter. Do we still have typewriters?"

"Yes. You know we have typewriters in the building." Houseman gestured for the door from which they had emerged. "You also know your way around the building."

Orson snapped his fingers. He put his hands on Koch's shoulder and led the young writer out of the room.

"Orson!" cried Paul Stewart. "We were working on that other script. What the Hell are we supposed to do now?"

"Oh, Paul," Orson said as he nearly had Koch out the door. It only marginally alarmed him that it took more than an instant for Orson to remember the actor's name. "You're on the clock; figure it out."

"Well," Houseman remarked. "I must say, I'm glad we have an ambulance on retainer."

*　　*　　*

It was well into the evening before Orson and Koch emerged from their seclusion. Koch's hands were arched and as red from typing as Orson's face. Rebecca followed them as well, and appeared to be bored without a laser-strewn battle amongst the stars to keep her occupied.

"Attention, ladies and gentlemen!" Orson said as he took to his broadcast podium and laid out several of the new pages. "Some lovely young ladies from the steno pool will be distributing the new copies in just a moment. Ah, there they are. I ask that you all remain flexible as we make changes over the course of the next day."

"A whole day of rehearsals with you, Orson?" Paul Stewart asked. "This *is* a luxury!"

Orson stopped what he was doing and glared at the culprit. He said nothing further. The ladies of the CBS steno pool handed out crisp, neat copies of the new script. As the performers and technicians of the Mercury Theatre looked over their new work, Orson headed straight for Dan Seymour. Although their last scuffle had been lifetimes ago for Orson, it must have been distressingly fresh for the announcer.

"You're not an actor, are you?" Orson asked.

The ad man shook his head and flinched as Orson moved closer with his arm extended. He grabbed Seymour's shoulder. "Have you ever wanted to *be* an actor?"

"No," Seymour croaked.

"Absolutely wonderful. Prepare to be made immortal. You are the unquestioned star of tomorrow night's performance," Orson informed Seymour and handed him one of the steno copies. "Read it just like you would any other copy you vomit out for any other broadcast.

"Koch!" Orson called out after he was satisfied that Seymour was left precisely where he needed to be:

absolutely bewildered.

"Y—yes, Orson?" Koch asked when it became clear that further hiding would be useless.

"The more I think about it, the location doesn't work for me. We'll need another town." Orson eyed him more intensely with every word.

"Location?" Koch asked. "What's wrong with Long Island?"

"It doesn't feel right. Change it to Grover's Mill."

"Where the Hell is Grover's Mill?"

"New Jersey."

"I'm not sure I get it."

Orson whipped around on Koch. "What?"

Koch froze in place. "I—I'm not sure I get it."

"You're not sure?" Orson asked. "Or you don't get it?"

"I—" Koch sounded as if he nearly choked on every word. "I don't get it."

"Good. Say what you mean, dear boy," Orson said. He turned his attention elsewhere.

"Does that mean we're not going to change it?"

"Unlikely. Housey!" he called out, leaving both Koch and Seymour to quietly shiver in the wake of what might have appeared to some to be a near-death experience. "I need to see if you can get Arturo's orchestra on short notice—"

"He won't work with you again after..." Houseman explained. "Well, after the incident—"

"Bah," Orson spat. He had no memory of the event to which Houseman referred, but that likely had nothing to do with any of the recent extraordinary events in his life.

"You broke a cello in half and did unholy things to a trombone. Also..."

"Pay him double," Orson ordered as he tried to reach for the next task on his elusive mental to-do list.

"That won't work," Houseman protested.

"Triple."

"Fine," Houseman ceded. "Will you accept Bernie if I can't make it happen?"

Orson nodded.

"That doesn't begin to solve our larger problem," Houseman said.

"Which is?"

*   *   *

"There is simply no way the Columbia Broadcastings System will allow the production of a program this startlingly—"

"Irresponsible?" Houseman offered. "At least, that's what I told him an hour ago before you got here."

"Yes! Irresponsible!" Davidson Taylor parroted.

"Just what the Hell is 'irresponsible' about it?" Orson asked. He was significantly less than engaged in the current conversation. He was far more consumed with the question of when precisely the program should shift perspectives and follow H.G. Wells' original first person narrative.

"Orson, I—" Taylor struggled over Orson's capacity to be intentionally obtuse.

"You propose to have the planet Mars invade the eastern seaboard in a mock news broadcast!" Houseman bellowed for what might have been the third time since the topic had originally been broached.

Off the executive's emphatic nod, Orson replied, "I know! It's fantastic, isn't it?" He turned to Rebecca, who despite having joined them for this conversation in the empty control room hadn't said much of anything. "It had been staring me in the face this whole time!"

"Don't look at me," Rebecca said. "I am as useless

around here as the writer."

"Orson," Houseman warned. "this gentleman is under no obligation to broadcast the program at all if the network feels ill at ease about it."

Orson groaned deeply and released every molecule of air from his lungs. "Fine," he told Houseman and then regarded Taylor earnestly. "We will put the standard intro at the top of the program. We will let the American People know that while the broadcast they are about to experience is unique in its innovation, the world is not truly being attacked by little green men.

"Now that I truly consider it..." Orson muttered and then snapped so that Koch knew he required his proximity. "That might pose a timing problem," he told the writer.

"I..." Koch, ever the wordsmith, offered by way of a plea for this nightmare to end already.

Orson snapped. "Wells... That is, the other Wells..." He laughed. "That is, *H.G.* Wells took an epoch to land his Martians. We'll just have to do it much sooner than that. It works out even better!"

"Why is it even better?" Koch asked.

"If we don't get to the invasion sooner, there's no way we'll be able to catch the armada off guard!"

"Orson..." Rebecca gently attempted to again remind him of his surroundings.

"The audience!" Orson corrected. "We won't be able to catch the audience off guard!" Taylor and Houseman shared a less than satisfied reaction to Orson's glee. "But not *too* off guard, of course."

Taylor smiled, the relief he felt present in his now slouched shoulder. "Thank you, Orson." He then went a step further than he had originally planned. "You know, despite what you might think, I like your program very much. It's a mark of prestige for the network to have such a literate and intellectual show on its airwaves."

Orson shook Taylor's hand. "You are a prince for saying so, my friend, and a head taller than your peers for recognizing such a fact. Now, if you'll excuse us, we have a great deal of work ahead of us."

"Of course, Orson," Taylor said. His tone betrayed the fact that he was completely unaware of Orson pushing him out the door.

"Does this mean we're going to have to re-write the whole damn thing?" Koch asked.

Orson's face raged at Koch's insolence. "Just the first ten minutes. Go. Now."

Koch was off in a flash, while Houseman's frown was deep enough to emerge in China. He never took his eyes off Orson. "No one's going to listen to our program in the first few minutes, Orson. They'll only switch to us when Bergen and his dummy take their first break."

Orson grinned. "Yes, that's right. You know, I completely forgot about that." He shrugged. "About time we put a ventriloquist dummy's radio show to good use, don't you think?"

"Goddammit," Housman muttered as he went to follow after Taylor.

"I wouldn't try too hard to catch up to him, Housey," Orson called after him. "You might get us all fired."

"Better than prison."

"They feed prisoners with some regularity. Our other options may not be so dignified."

Houseman had no reply aside from his own exit. He didn't move much farther than that, and instead stewed in the studio on the other side of the soundproof glass. He may have had further choice words for Orson, but the glass filtered those thoughts from any sensitive ears. Still giggling from the exchange, Orson's amusement eventually came to a halt when he realized his only current companion, Rebecca, did not share in his glee.

"Now I suppose it's your turn to tell me this isn't going to work," Orson barked.

"I don't even know what 'this' is," Rebecca said.

"The cycle is starting all over again, don't you see?"

Rebecca rose from her seat and finally looked at Orson directly. "Let's say the cycle is restarting with iteration one, which I don't believe. Let's say you somehow convince the United States military that New Jersey is the target of invaders from Mars, which I'd hazard to guess that no one, including you, is that dumb. How is the technology of 1938 supposed to withstand an attack from a people thousands of years more advanced?"

"On one hand, we'll have the element of surprise," Orson maintained.

"And the other?"

"If I'm right, and all of this is starting all over again, they'll only be hundreds of years ahead of us."

Rebecca's face remained unwilling to offer any clue as to her inner feeling about the desperate plan. "Fine, we'll do it your way. If for no other reason than I can't even begin to think of anything else we could try."

"Oh, Rebecca," Orson crooned as he grasped her hands. "You've made me so happy."

The physical intimacy of the gesture seemed so unnatural that Rebecca pulled her hands away immediately.

"Stop that," she said. "You're like a brother to me."

"A younger brother," Orson corrected.

Rebecca's grimace deepened.

\*     \*     \*

# TUESDAY, NOVEMBER 16, 2141

# 7:01 PM COORDINATED MARTIAN TIME
# ITERATION 1
# MARTIAN ARCH I (IN TRANSIT)
# KAN-UR'S FLAGSHIP

As the waves of light flashed across his ship's main windows, Kan-ur nursed a quiet suspicion that the Arch was not a doorway to the past at all, but actually a portal to some deeper reckoning he had not previously considered. Was God beyond this torrent of light? The Devil? Was the arch the largest snake oil remedy in human history? Was the electrical discharge of the Arch no sort of portal at all, and all that would greet him on the other side would be the same rotted Earth and overactive Mars he had always known.

That seemed to be the most likely answer as the distortion around his ship dissipated. The cosmos around Mars seemed unchanged from the Mars they had left. The only immediate sign that anything was different was the sudden absence of the human influence on the red planet.

With no further sign that the trip to the past had worked, Kan-ur quickly became aware that he had been holding his breath since the journey had begun.

"Come about," he ordered the Pilot.

He shifted his controls, and the crammed control deck's main window swirled around them. Kan-ur nearly leapt from his seat. He had never expected—hoped to avoid, might have been more apt—to be leading this expedition. And yet, here he was, staring at a still, blue-green Earth. It wasn't a photograph. It wasn't a distortion of the truth. It was a live magnification of the planet of his forebears. The earth was alive and so close; Kan-ur could almost touch it.

On its face, Kan-ur was relieved to learn that from

their vantage point, millions of kilometers away, everything seemed in order.

"What do we have?" Kan-ur asked.

The Radio Technician looked at her instruments. "I'm picking up radio signals that would indicate we've emerged in the year... 1938."

Kan-ur might have hoped for a primordial world before humanity began sullying the air, but with a large population of indigenous humans more than willing to destroy themselves of their own accord, he would have to improvise.

"They won't know what hit them," the Pilot remarked.

"Quiet," Kan-ur ordered. "There is still much that could go wrong."

Once Kan-ur conclusively determined that conditions on Earth were as he anticipated, he was to send word of an all-clear back through the distortion. If Kan-ur had calculated correctly, the distortion would stay open for another six hours. He intended to use that time fully and do several sweeps of the inhabited planet.

The world in front of Kan-ur was too busy fighting a war or starving to death to notice that he was about cleanse them of their strife. It would be a mercy killing, one that would ensure the survival of their descendants. If Kan-ur presented the information just that way to the people of the alive Earth beyond, they may just surrender willingly. He'd need a better natural communicator to sell that notion, but that would have to wait. He wasn't about to put anything to chance. The invasion would proceed as planned.

A single alarm went off on the Pilot's control console. It wasn't a particularly harsh or insistent alert. The beeping was far too discordant with the normal symphony coming from the ship. Kan-ur couldn't help but notice.

"What's that?" Kan-ur asked.

The Radio Technician pulled her attention to the data surrounding the alert. "Wait a minute..." she said, re-checking the figures. "That can't be right..."

"What?" Kan-ur asked again. "*What* can't be right?"

"It didn't show up initially, so I'm guessing here, but it appears to be hooked into our power output node and is just now coming online, but it doesn't look like anything I've ever seen."

"What?" Kan-ur repeated a third time, although the unlikely answer was becoming clear.

"There's another ship down there on the planet," she revealed.

Kan-ur clenched his teeth and wondered how long an investigation into this near-impossibility would take, and whether he should wait to have re-enforcements sent through the arch.

"How did it get there?" Kan-ur asked.

"I have no idea," the Radio Technician said, struggling to make further sense—or any sense—of her readings.

The Pilot turned to Kan-ur. "You don't suppose it's from—?"

"Another world?" Kan-ur asked with contempt. "Don't be preposterous. There are no such things as extra-terrestrials. Even if there were, the time and energy necessary to travel to the planet Earth would make the journey inefficient to the point of insanity."

The Pilot returned to his control, thoroughly chastised, but unable to offer any other explanation.

"Where is this craft?" Kan-ur asked after a moment when he too reconsidered the possibility of visitors from another solar system.

"North America. Eastern section. A town called Grover's Mill. It's just a few miles east of Princeton University," the Radio Technician responded.

"New Jersey..." Kan-ur whispered disbelievingly. "Then we shall go there directly," Kan-ur told the Pilot. He rose from his seat and spoke into the ship's public address system. "Attention. The great day for humanity is finally here. Our homecoming is nigh and our great work will begin in... Grover's Mill, New Jersey."

Kan-ur could hear both from the ship's internal communication system and through the deck below him the celebrations of his men. They hadn't noticed, or had simply stopped listening before Kan-ur hesitated with their destination. This was for the best; Kan-ur could now be left alone to think about how this did not feel right.

Their new leader might have called the whole invasion off if he could receive live radio transmissions from Earth. The man behind one of those signals was already hard at work destroying his plans. And thankfully, at that particular moment, no one was listening.

# CHAPTER THIRTEEN

SUNDAY, OCTOBER 30TH, 1938
8:01 PM EST
ITERATION ZERO
ALL ACROSS THE COLUMBIA BROADCASTING
SYSTEM
EARTH

"The Columbia Broadcasting System and its affiliated stations present Orson Welles and the Mercury Theatre on the Air in *The War of The Worlds* by H.G. Wells!"

Tchaikovsky's Piano Concerto in B-flat minor filled the studio as all other activity came to a sudden stop. The Tchaikovsky piece always produced a visceral, nervous reaction in Orson. He had no fear of performance in general. It was—especially now—the only thing in all of creation that he did not fear one whit. However, when that music began, things were different. This program had his name on it, right at the start of the broadcast. More so than *The Shadow* ever could be, this was *his* show.

There was also the small matter of the fate of the Earth and its myriad futures hanging in the balance, but that was a secondary concern.

Dan Seymour continued his opening of the program, but with a wary eye on Orson the entire time. "Ladies and Gentlemen, the director of the Mercury Theatre and star of these broadcasts—"

Orson lunged at the announcer, but the gesture was pure artifice. It stopped the announcer for only a half a beat, but for the rest of the evening he would be both pristinely aware of what was happening around him, and completely terrified. This was Orson's design. If the remainder of the American population proved as malleable as Seymour, then this just might work.

"—Orson Welles."

He attacked his copy without hesitation. "No one would have believed that this world was being watched keenly and closely by intelligences greater than man's and yet as mortal as his own..."

\*　　\*　　\*

8:03 PM EST
PRINCETON OBSERVATORY
PRINCETON, NEW JERSEY

"Because he's funny!" Jimmy said.

"Yes," William, Jimmy's father said. "But the question I'm asking you is why you prefer to listen to a ventriloquist on the radio. It's an auditory medium."

The boy looked sour. He may not have comprehended the conundrum, but he made no effort to hide his feelings about his father's intransigence.

"Very well," William surrendered. "Charlie McCarthy it is. You may set the dial."

Jimmy leapt for the radio and snapped it on. His

previous sourness disappeared just as quickly as it first appeared. He practically vibrated with impatience as the unit glowed with the warming of its tubes and the air filled with just enough ozone to not alarm, but instead give the atmosphere an almost cozy quality.

The observatory at Princeton University was virtually ignored even on busy days. Observance of celestial bodies was sufficiently looked down upon in an age where the world's most celebrated astronaut went by the name of Buck and was kid's stuff, even by Jimmy's standards. On the Sunday before Hallowe'en, the place was a tomb.

Jimmy pleaded with his father to come along to the telescope to log routine celestial observances. William relented with the proviso that Jimmy act on his best behavior during the process, a bargain his son had so far failed to fulfill. With Edgar Bergen and his dummy now drafted for nanny duty, William had a fighting chance to get some work done.

And yet, as his son's laughter filled the domed observation deck, there remained a longing in William to take this opportunity to spend more time with the boy. Jimmy's incessant questions about his father's work were no longer the source of William's distraction; the fact that he enjoyed being a father far more than his work as an astronomy professor ruined his productivity for the evening.

"How's the show so far?" William called down to the lower level of the observatory. He could only hear the dim roar of the broadcast from his elevation.

"Pretty good," Jimmy called up.

"I'll be right down," William said. He'd find nothing new in the sky tonight.

\*    \*    \*

8:07 PM EST
FORT DIX ARMY AIR FORCE BASE
BURLINGTON COUNTY, NEW JERSEY

The Officer of the Watch turned off the radio quickly, but knew that the Watch Commander had already seen and heard the Officer's malfeasance. The Commander smiled, and placed two Pepsi-Cola's on the watch desk. "It's all right, Bobby. Even Hitler has enough decency not to invade on a Sunday night." The Commander walked back to his office, taking one of the drinks for himself. "What were you listening to?"

"Edgar Bergen and Charlie McCarthy," the Officer replied.

"Turn it up so I can hear it, will ya?" the Commander asked, and then added, "Do you suppose he bothers to not move his lips when he does the radio show?"

The officer seriously contemplated the question before answering. "How can we be sure he even has the Dummy with him?" he asked.

"Show folk..." the Commander lamented as he sat down.

*　　*　　*

8:25 PM EST
RADIO CITY MUSIC HALL
MANHATTAN, NY

Edgar Bergen always had his dummy, Charlie McCarthy, with him when he broadcast *The Chase and Sandborn Hour*, and he *never* moved his lips while Charlie spoke. Bergen had a live audience in front of him who had no sense that the format was a touch preposterous for his act. Also, it would be rude to try to interrupt Charlie when he spoke.

About twenty minutes into the program, Edgar took his first break of the evening. As the orchestra played their first interlude, Bergen would never realize that his ability to keep a rigidly focused show schedule may have just saved the earth, and in fact all possible Earths, from fiery destruction. For his own part, Bergen was merely trying to put on a good show.

\*     \*     \*

8:25 PM EST
CBS RADIO BUILDING
MANHATTAN, NEW YORK

Across town, a good show was only one of Orson Welles' concerns. Besides the matters of cosmic significance that only he and Rebecca knew of and Houseman flatly rejected, he was now a man named Pierson, and his concern for the stars and planets closer to Earth veered to the mundane. He was also keeping an eye on one particular member of the Mercury Company.

Paul Stewart—the imminently competent actor who had been so thoughtlessly dismissed as rehearsal director for this broadcast—stood near a radio in the studio. He listened intently to another broadcast through a large headset. Stewart and Orson had not broken eye contact since the Mercury's broadcast began.

Stewart flailed his arms so Orson would notice. Orson gave a cue for Dan Seymour to stand ready, and gave a second signal to another actor, Frank Readick. Their current scene together would be cut short.

\*   \*   \*

8:26 PM EST
PRINCETON OBSERVATORY
PRINCETON, NEW JERSEY

"Aww, shucks," Jimmy said as Bergen's orchestra began their number. "I hate it when the music starts playing. Nothing's ever funny about music."

Noting his son's education may need further broadening, William reached for the dial. "Perhaps another program will provide sufficient stimulation," Jimmy's heartbroken countenance when William found a signal on WCBS did not go unnoticed. "We'll turn back in a minute, I assure you."

"The chances against anything manlike on Mars are a million to one," the Princeton Astronomer—a man named Pierson—explained over the radio.

Silence passed between father and son as this program—whatever it was—went to its own musical break. This was until Jimmy brought to voice the one issue that had been on their minds.

"But daddy," the boy said, "Your name isn't Pierson."

Both father and son were sufficiently intrigued by CBS' current program. They were unlikely to return to Edgar Bergen any time soon.

\*   \*   \*

8:27 PM EST
FORT DIX ARMY AIR FORCE BASE
BURLINGTON COUNTY, NEW JERSEY

"Go ahead and change back," the Watch Commander insisted from his office.

"Just a second," the Officer belted back as he turned the radio up.

The Commander sprang out of his office in a flash, ready and willing to break his soda bottle and use it in his pursuit to reclaim unit discipline.

"What was that, Lieutenant?"

The Officer leapt from his seat. "Just a second, *sir*," he barked, but with a far cry more respect than he had exhibited the first time.

The broadcast continued reporting the details of the fallen Martian object's sudden collision with a farm in Grover's Mill. Perplexed, the Officer had to consult a nearby map to confirm the nearly-unknown town was several miles from Princeton.

"Did you hear anything?" the Commander asked.

The Officer shook his head. "Wouldn't somebody have called you?"

"Yeah..." the Commander agreed. "Must be some kind of new play they're doing," he remarked as he headed back to the office. "Switch it back to Edgar Bergen, will ya?"

"Can I leave it on this for another minute?"

"I don't really care," the Commander admitted. "I can barely hear it anyway."

\*   \*   \*

8:27 PM EST
CBS RADIO BUILDING
SECOND FLOOR
MANHATTAN, NEW YORK

Several hundred thousand miles below the currently

hatching Martian invasion, and about a hundred miles away from the fictional location of that incursion, someone called into the network's switchboards. Several someones, actually.

Moments after the fictional Martian cylinder from H.G. Wells novel rained destruction down on the one part of the planet that actually had a functioning flying saucer, the network switchboard came alive with light.

There were the people looking to confirm The Mercury's broadcast was a work of fiction, which the operators were happy to assure them it was without transferring them any further. Those calls were odd, but ultimately manageable. As the destruction continued across the Eastern Seaboard, the calls got stranger. There were far more calls from affiliates, frantically trying to come up with some answer more forceful than it was just a show. Some listeners had relatives in the area of Grover's Mill, and inquired if the network had a list of casualties.

After disconnecting from one of the more frantic calls, one of the operators turned pleadingly to her supervisor. "Should somebody put a call in high up with the network?" she asked.

The supervisor coldly assessed the condition of the call board and was unimpressed. "We can handle it," the supervisor stated flatly.

\*     \*     \*

8:28 PM EST
PRINCETON OBSERVATORY
PRINCETON, NJ

William felt ridiculous, and yet there he was, standing once again on the observation platform, contemplating the impossible.

He approached the telescope after he convinced himself that he was doing so simply to log the data he had been assigned to monitor. He could proceed if he was not looking for fantastical monstrosities from the Red Planet.

He wished he hadn't looked at all.

Roughly 1.5 million miles from the outer boundaries of the atmosphere—and approaching the speed of light—a long metallic cylinder barreled towards the Earth.

The various elements of machinery attached to the object's form, the light emanating from it, and what appeared to be some sort of exhaust trailing out of the craft all pointed to one conclusion:

The object was man made, and it was headed straight for New Jersey.

And somehow, someone on the CBS News Service claimed to have William's job, and had managed to come to the same conclusion as recently as ten minutes ago.

\*   \*   \*

8:35 PM EST
FORT DIX ARMY AIR FORCE BASE
BURLINGTON COUNTY, NEW JERSEY

"Fella, you have placed a call with an Army Air Force Base," the Officer of the Watch told the telephone receiver. "I can tell you we are in no mood—"

The Commander emerged from his office to silently assess the commotion of the only call they had received all evening.

"Are you pulling my leg?" the Officer further pried. "You're—you're not?" He finally looked up at the Commander, letting the person on the other end of the connection rattle on. "You may need to take this, sir."

"Who is it?" the Commander asked with more mirth than the moment might have otherwise called for. "The President?"

The Officer shook his head. "It's an astronomer from Princeton."

"What, like on the radio?"

The Officer didn't quite shake his head, but he didn't nod either.

"What does he want?" the Commander asked.

"I'm going to let you talk to him," the officer said, handing the receiver over.

\* \* \*

8:37 PM EST
CBS RADIO BUILDING
MAIN ENTRANCE
MANHATTAN, NEW YORK

When Taylor left the Dewey fundraiser long before the festivities ended, to say he was surprised by the subject of the telephone call would have been an understatement, no matter how much it shouldn't have fazed him in the slightest.

He emerged from the taxi and marched quickly into the building. The switchboard supervisor waited for him. A throng of panicky people were also present, but he made a concerted effort not to look them in the eye.

"The switchboard has been at capacity for the last twenty minutes; my ladies cannot keep up with it, Mr. Taylor."

"Ma'am, I've already gotten a call from the President of the Network asking me to put a stop to the invaders from

Mars. Rest assured, I will take care of your problems in due course, but I do have other priorities this evening."

\* \* \*

While Seymour prepared to give the performance of a lifetime, a toxic cloud engulfed all of Manhattan. Meanwhile, Orson Welles was fighting for his life.

"I absolutely will not!" Orson rasped.

"You will cut into the air for station identification and a reminder that this program is fiction, or I will call officers here to arrest you for trespassing," Taylor retorted, now completely inoculated to Orson's charms.

Orson laughed and then looked at Houseman, standing silent several feet away. "Wouldn't that be the most wonderful publicity?"

"Orson..." Houseman admonished.

"Shut up!" Orson snapped at him, finally finding the man's attempt to mother him just too much to handle. Orson's only sense of doubt came from the realization that nearby Rebecca did not seem enthused with the progress of the evening.

"Test me, and you will absolutely regret it." Taylor then moved to make good on his threat.

Orson rolled his eyes and moved back to the studio, confident that Taylor barely had the power to order around a shoe shiner, much less him. And yet, Rebecca's clear disapproval forced him to stop.

"What?" Orson asked her.

"You've already done what you came here to do," Rebecca warned. "Everyone, including the authorities are looking up at the skies. You and I really need to get going."

"Will someone call an ambulance?!" Orson called out to the control room.

Taylor looked confused as he furiously scribbled something on paper; Rebecca only more so.

"Nonsense," Orson assured her as he resumed his move to make his cue.

"Why?" she called after him.

"Every single radio is tuned to me, if you think for one moment I'm going to let this go, you're absolutely mad."

\*　　\*　　\*

8:40 PM EST
PRINCETON OBSERVATORY
PRINCETON, NEW JERSEY

*"Thick streamers of black smoke shot with threads of red fire were driving up into the still air, and throwing dark shadows upon the green treetops eastward... Apparently the Martians were setting fire to everything within range of their Heat-Ray."*

A harsh whine nearly blew out the speaker. Silence dotted with stray chirps of static filled the airwaves for a stretch that felt like the eternity one might wait at the Pearly Gates.

"Dad," Jimmy cut through the silence. "Why aren't we dead?"

William had no answer. He was far too confused to speak. He only hoped there was someone on God's green earth—was it even green anymore?—that could make this all not so.

\*　　\*　　\*

8:43 PM EST
CBS RADIO STUDIO
MANHATTAN, NEW YORK

With a thud that no one would ever realize was Orson Welles throwing his shoes on the sound effects table, Dan Seymour died on the air and concluded the only performance of his career. Far more interested performers than he would search their whole life for an opportunity of similar potential and never come close.

Orson stretched his face, preparing to re-claim the spotlight. Paul Stewart, back now in the fold of the broadcast, offered the final bit of verisimilitude the program needed before Orson would try to calm the crowd down, not because the network insisted upon it, but because the broadcast needed *some* sense of catharsis in order to be effective.

"Isn't there anyone on the air?" Stewart continued. "Isn't there anyone on the air? Isn't there anyone— 2X2L—" Stewart's haunting voice called out to a connection that would never answer. Filling Orson's eyes red with fury, Taylor chose this moment to enter the studio and menacingly hand a piece of paper to Seymour.

Orson gave Stewart the cue to stop and was ready with his other hand to give Bernie the cue to bring the orchestra to bear, but then Seymour reverted to his true nature.

"You are listening to a CBS presentation of Orson Welles and the Mercury Theatre on the Air in an original dramatization of *The War of the Worlds* by H.G. Wells. The performance will continue after a brief intermission."

Orson flung his pages off the podium and lunged for Taylor. Orson grabbed the barely-man by the neck as the orchestra resumed its Tchaikovsky.

"I'm going to kill you," Orson whispered to the executive.

# CHAPTER FOURTEEN

SUNDAY, OCTOBER 30, 1938
8:45 PM EST
ITERATION ZERO
KAN-UR'S FLAGSHIP
FIFTEEN MILES ABOVE GROVER'S MILL, NEW
JERSEY

"The closer we get, the stranger it becomes," Kan-ur's Pilot reported as they cleared the outer bounds of Earth's atmosphere. "It's unlike any ship I've ever seen or even heard of in the records, but it is clearly responding to our power signal."

"So it's not one of our ships, but for some reason, its computer and equipment think it is," Kan-ur assessed.

"But how could that be? Could there have been another group that fled Earth and are attempting the same process?"

"Unlikely. How would that ship down there get through the security measures and get through the arch without us noticing?"

"Could people have had that kind of technology in

1938?"

Kan-ur might have laughed if such a reaction would have not been such a grave violation of decorum. "Humans of this age have a thirst for wanton destruction and access to some rudimentary machinery to slake that thirst, but they lack refinement."

Somewhere in the middle of Kan-ur's ruminations, he looked at the clock on the control room's far bulkhead. It indicated that the rift would collapse in just over three hours' time. There was still time; but this side trip had made him nervous.

"Chairman, I'm receiving a transmission," the Radio Technician reported.

Kan-ur continued to look at the clock. "You should be receiving a litany of transmissions."

"Yes, sir, but I think you are going to want to hear this one."

Kan-ur waved his hand. The Technician punched the errant signal through to the control room's speakers. In frantic tones a news reporter brought word of invaders from Mars and the destruction that followed them.

"How could they know we're coming?" The Pilot appeared so completely stricken by the question that the ship veered off of its course without his focused vigilance.

"They couldn't," Kan-ur said softly. A far more unfortunate question ran through his mind. Could the ship in Grover's Mill be from another world? If so, how did radio broadcasters of the age come to these conclusions before he did?

The clock blinked off and then almost immediately returned. Nearly all of the Pilot's alarms were going off at the same time. A dull vibration echoed through the ship.

"What happened?" Kan-ur asked.

"There are a number of military vehicles and

equipment converging on our proposed landing site; they have brought their weapons to bear."

Kan-ur descended into his seat. "Activate weapons systems," he commanded. The weaponry that the military forces had brought to this place, this Grover's Mill—how could they have been alerted at all?—were unequal to the task of defeating his own war machines, and yet he couldn't help looking at that clock.

The battle for the future of humanity had begun.

\*     \*     \*

8:55 PM EST
CBS RADIO BUILDING
MANHATTAN, NEW YORK

The battle for the future of the Mercury Theatre on The Air drew quickly to a close.

Orson recovered his composure quickly enough to resume his post and carry on with his final monologue as Professor Pierson of Princeton University.

Towards the end of the broadcast, a few events of extreme import to the future of Orson Welles occurred. First, two uniformed officers of the New York Police Department entered the studio control room and flanked Davidson Taylor. This development did not diminish Orson's contempt for the man, but it did add an air of begrudging respect to the proceedings. Second, Rebecca slammed a piece of paper onto the control room window while Pierson shared a brief exchange with a stranger amidst the Martian ruin. It read:

YOUR AMBULANCE IS HERE     ?

The question mark was far enough away from the main text that it was possible the message was a statement and the punctuation was more parenthetical commentary.

None of it mattered to Orson, ultimately. The show had reached its natural crescendo.

"Now we see further," Pierson via Orson explained, hoping that his next words would put to rest the horrifying ideas he had introduced this evening so that he could actually vanquish them in peace.

"If the Martians can reach Venus, there is no reason to suppose that the thing is impossible for men, and when the slow cooling of the sun makes this earth uninhabitable, as at last it must do, it may be that the thread of life that has begun here will have streamed out and caught our sister planet within its toils.

"Dim and wonderful is the vision I have conjured up in my mind of life spreading slowly from this little seed bed of the Solar System throughout the inanimate vastness of sidereal space. But that is a remote dream. It may be, on the other hand, that the destruction of the Martians is only a reprieve. To them, and not to us, is the future ordained."

Never taking his hate-filled eyes from Taylor, Orson reached for the last page of his copy. Bernie and his orchestra played again.

He eyed his copy as the orchestra died down. He then began what would likely be his farewell to the American people, all at the wizened old age of twenty-three.

"This is Orson Welles, ladies and gentlemen, out of character to assure you that *The War of The Worlds* has no further significance than as the holiday offering it was intended to be: the Mercury Theatre's own radio version of dressing up in a sheet and jumping out of a bush and saying 'Boo!'.

"We annihilated the world before your very ears and

utterly destroyed the CBS," he pointed at Taylor, safe in his cocoon in the control booth, and then dragged his finger across his neck. "You will be relieved, I hope, to learn that we didn't mean it, and that both institutions are still open for business."

Taylor got the message, and retreated quietly back into the recesses of the control room with his thugs. One immovable object out of the way, Orson continued his farewell address. "So, everybody, goodbye, and remember that terrible lesson you learned tonight. That grinning, glowing globular invader of your living room is an inhabitant of the pumpkin patch, and if your doorbell rings and nobody's there, that was no Martian... It's merely Hallowe'en."

Orson snapped his fingers and Bernie's orchestra kicked into gear to close out the program, with the strangely apt assistance of one Mister Daniel Seymour. In another life, Orson may have stayed behind to bathe in the restless adulation of his theatrical company. Each of them knew that while they may still come to be involved with superior productions—especially if they continued to follow their wunderkind director—the work they did this evening would rank among their finest. Orson headed out the door with Rebecca in tow before Seymour's final tag concluded. Taylor and his temporary bodyguards had insufficient time to realize that Orson was leaving, and were unlikely to be able to stop him if they did.

As always, it would be left to John Houseman to clean up any messes Orson Welles left behind.

\*     \*     \*

9:07 PM EST
ROUTE 27

## BRUNSWICK COUNTY, NEW JERSEY
## EARTH, IN CASE YOU WERE WONDERING

The sight of an ambulance with its sirens blaring was a relatively common occurrence on Route 27. They were usually headed east towards the far superior hospitals in New York City, but there were never Manhattan ambulances driving *into* the state. Indeed, on this particular evening the vehicle taking Orson and Rebecca back to their crash site would just barely make the top five strangest sights in New Jersey. People would have assumed correctly that their presence must have had something to do with invading Martians.

As they rode, Orson lamented the lack of a standard radio in the ambulance, but reviews would have to wait.

"So, my friend," Rebecca said breezily. "What do you want to do tomorrow night?"

Orson shrugged.

"I'll tell you," she said. "The same thing we do every night: try to save the world."

Orson was far more optimistic. He assumed neither of them would live to see November, and would therefore never have to go through this process again.

Rebecca's answer was interrupted by a sharp electric whine coming from her satchel. She examined the bag's contents, and removed two sidearms that had previously belonged to October's army. When the power had gone out on the *Oneida*, the weapons had similarly gone dark. They were now glowing with intense yellow light. She handed one of the weapons to Orson, who made a half-hearted attempt to beg off.

"Don't get squeamish on me now, Welles," Rebecca warned him. "We never would have gotten this far if it weren't for you."

He took the weapon and grinned sheepishly, never before looking more like a man in his early twenties than he did in that moment.

"They ain't gonna let us go any further," the driver said once it had become clear to all parties involved that they had come to a stop. Orson thought about arguing with the man, considering the amount he was being paid for the impromptu taxi service, but Rebecca had already jumped out of the back of the vehicle and was making a run for the field beyond. Orson followed.

When they arrived at their crash site just over twenty minutes later, it appeared as if they had already lost. The military vehicles called in to investigate the problems on this Jersey farm valiantly flung any and all explosive devices they had at their disposal, but to no avail. Kan-ur's long, landed ship—which only occupied a dim memory in the back of Orson's mind—let loose with a volley of yellow energy that only the human tanks could withstand.

"We have to get back to the ship!" Rebecca called out in between attempts to fire off shots at the new ship. "We can probably draw their fire!"

The vibrations on the ground below them only intensified as the large ship began to take off. Orson looked to Rebecca. "Now what?" he screamed.

"Get to the ship anyway! We need to make sure they don't come back!"

Orson followed her dutifully. When they arrived at the *Oneida V*, the small silo that had broken its fall yesterday had evaporated under Kan-ur's barrage. The ship itself appeared to be largely unharmed. They boarded it and with power returned to the ship's machinery, Rebecca initiated liftoff and followed the fleeing vessel.

\* \* \*

9:01 PM EST
GROVER'S MILL, NEW JERSEY
EARTH, FOR THE MOMENT

The battle between the native forces and Kan-ur's efforts raged on, if a tad lopsidedly. After the fifth glance at the perpetually ticking clock in half as many minutes, Kan-ur rose from his chair. "Provide suppressive fire," he ordered. "I am going to investigate that ship myself."

"But, sir," the Pilot protested. Kan-ur was already gone.

After marching through the night air tinged with the stark ozone of their battle fire, Kan-ur entered the mystery ship, and his confusion only worsened. It was somehow recognizable as technology he should be aware of, but he didn't have the first clue as to how to operate the controls. Two dead bodies were at either end of the cockpit. One looked to be a normal human who had died on impact. The body in the other corner of might have once been human, but that gave the husk the benefit of the doubt. Both had been dead several days by the smell of it. The carnage didn't help Kan-ur's critical thinking skills in the slightest. It all lead to some distressing conclusion he couldn't quite attain. He activated his communication unit. "Prepare to return to the rift point; I will follow you back in the mystery ship."

Before the man got a chance to attempt his incorrect best guess, two of the natives cut through the maelstrom beyond and boarded the ship. He quickly moved behind a bulkhead and out of sight. Furthering his confusion, the mystery beyond limits Kan-ur previously thought possible, one of these native – the woman – appeared to be well-versed in the operation of the craft.

As the woman piloted the craft expertly into the night

sky, Kan-ur leveled his sidearm at the seated man—who seemed oddly superfluous to the current proceedings—and attempted to get their attention.

*   *   *

Orson leapt from his seat as the upper headrest exploded in fire. Rebecca quickly put the craft on autopilot as she too whipped around and leveled her weapon at a ghost. The man, with his aquiline features and faux aristocratic bearing was nothing less than a younger version of the despot that lay dead only a few feet away from them.

"My questions are as follows," the younger Kan-ur said in a voice free of the technological obfuscations that had so thoroughly dehumanized his older self. "What is this ship? Who are you people? And who are they?" he asked, pointing to the two corpses.

"I'll answer the final question first," Rebecca said. "The answer may shed light on your other inquiries. That man I've never seen before in my life, but that creature on the floor is you."

Kan-ur looked stricken at both Rebecca and Orson.

"I know how you feel," Orson remarked.

The intruder neglected follow-ups, the implications of Rebeca's answer just beginning to dawn on him. "It is of vital importance that you pilot this craft to follow my own ship. We are headed back to the planet Mars to alert your descendants that it is safe to come through a temporal distortion. If you cooperate, I can assure you that no harm will come to you."

Rebecca laughed. It may have been the first time she had ever done so. "Well! I can't believe I'm ever going to say this, but thank you, Lord Chairman," then louder, she added, "Schmoogle Boogle!"

The electronic assistant appeared from the wall projectors and bowed to Rebecca. "Hi! I'm Schmoogle Boogle! I'm your friendly internet search engine. How can I help?"

In Kan-ur's continued shock, Rebecca was able to consider the phantom's question more fully. "Fire all weapons systems!" she ordered.

"Sounds like fun! You've got it!" Schmoogle Boogle cried as their ship came to life, shooting yellow beams of destruction in all directions for several seconds. Out in the cosmos beyond the port holes, Kan-ur's ship broke apart like cheap fireworks.

In a rage, Kan-ur once again opened fire in the cabin. He was able to get a shot off in Schmoogle Boogle's direction. The shot hit S.B.'s generators and processors, causing the sweet prince of helpfulness to explode in light. Even Kan-ur could tell that the strange ghost would never return.

Regaining some of his composure, he then fired at Rebecca. The shot went into her mid-section, but did not emerge. She felt warmer than she ever thought possible. Her mouth tasted like blood.

In a few short moments, Rebecca would be the first person Kan-ur had ever killed. In the moment he took to fire the fatal shot, he realized he had no trouble taking any other lives in pursuit of his goals. He whipped around towards Orson. "Do you have any idea what you two have done?" You have *destroyed* humanity's only chance to survive!"

Between agonizing over Rebecca's heated attempts to catch her breath and failing, Orson looked at Kan-ur. "I can't believe I'm going to have the chance to tell you again, but the world will be just fine without you, sir! We'll adapt! We'll go on! The only way forward is not to repeat the past over and over again, but to move forward!"

Kan-ur primed his weapon once more, and Orson knew this was the end, but he took some small comfort in the knowledge that Kan-ur would have a great deal of difficulty saving the race in his own small, stupid way using only a spaceship he had never seen before and could never hope to fly correctly;. Doing so was Orson's job and his job alone.

"Orson... Hold on..." Rebecca cried out weakly as her hand hovered over a large red button that Orson recognized as the decompression control she had admonished him about lifetimes ago.

Orson leapt for the partially singed chair. Klaxons filled the cabin as air fled his lungs. Orson would never be entirely sure as his world spent those five seconds collapsing around him, but the vacuum of space swallowed Rebecca, Goodman, and both Kan-urs and spit them out into the fiery wreck of the younger Kan-ur's ship. With Rebecca's hand pulled away from the decompression control, the ship began the process of re-sealing and repressurizing itself.

Orson felt air re-enter his lungs slowly, but not fast enough to keep him from drifting asleep. He had no idea where he'd go next. He expected he was following Rebecca, wherever it was that she was going.

\*　　\*　　\*

THREE-HUNDRED AND THIRTY-THREE YEARS LATER
TUESDAY, NOVEMBER 16, 2241
11:01 PM COORDINATED MARTIAN TIME
ITERATION ZERO
OLYMPUS MONS, MARS

The time had passed. Those left behind by Kan-ur held out hope for as long as they could. Ten minutes after the deadline with no word, they knew the attempt had failed. Were Kan-ur still alive, he would have made contact. His death in the electronic maelstrom created by the arch was far more likely.

Many panicked. Most thought all was lost, that the abject discomfort of human life on the planet Mars would guarantee that humanity would live out their final days on the Red Planet, slowly gasping for breathing room.

As time went on, several in the Olympus institute began to grow enamored of an item that had been largely deemed a myth: The October Archive.

Using the information and theories obtained within, humanity was able to carve out a sustainable life for itself on Mars. Earth may never have been able to support people again, but life carried on.

It was as if whoever created The October Archive generations ago knew that life on Mars would be humanity's destiny, and spent considerable resources preparing for that eventuality.

\*     \*     \*

MONDAY, OCTOBER 31, 1938
1:02 AM
ITERATION ZERO
SOMEWHERE

*Orson Welles was dead. It was the only explanation for the sight ahead of him. He stood on a crimson mountain, overseeing an army of over three hundred men.*

*Each one of the three-hundred had some version of his own face.*

*Most were old. Nearly all looked hardened by strife. Some seemed disappointed with Kan-ur's demise. One had major head trauma and appeared thoroughly confused.*

*October—that is, the man Orson had most recently come to know as October—stood next to him, assessing their forces.*

*"It's done," October said.*

*Orson tried to speak, but no words came.*

*"The cycle has been broken. Now go, Orson Welles, and live the life we had no opportunity to pursue. Follow your passions. Be extraordinary. But above all, do this: Forget us. Do not be October. He is a man of war who came from a planet named for war, and can only fulfill one purpose."*

*"War?" Orson finally spoke, although it may have been the words of every Orson assembled.*

*October nodded. "Yours must be a higher purpose."*

*Orson tried to ask what that might be, but without the support of the other Orsons, he was unable to form further words.*

*   *   *

When Orson came to, his head ached and darkness was all around him. He may very well have been dead. He was still on the *Oneida V*, but that was only a marginally good sign. Grasping in the dark, Orson managed to find the large red button that had finally put the human race back on track only a few short hours ago. Although the ship's power supply had once again slipped away after Kan-ur's ship exploded, the mechanics of the decompression hatch still worked. The door open and spit Orson out into whatever lay beyond.

The ship was wedged into the Earth – and it indeed was the Earth – but this time Orson was positive it would never fly again. He figured the ship had once again crash landed, only this time on some locale far from civilization.

Despair taking over, he fell to his knees. Why had he not left the broadcast sooner? Had he done so, his prospects might have been better. As it stood, he was likely once again at the mercy of one of the plethora of despots the world now offered with no waiting. Rebecca might still be alive. As it stood, there would be no reprieve from the loss filling Orson in that moment. She would be dead forever.

The night sky was above him and air filled his lungs without any assistance. A road sign down the way read: MOUNT PROSPECT – 9 miles.

He was home. Better than that, he was wrong. He was so close to human civilization, he could almost taste it. Orson Welles, after all of his improbable journey, was back in Illinois.

He laughed upward, taunting those that might once have brought him down. He walked in the direction of the sign, quietly mulling potential options for what he could do with the crashed ship behind him. He needed to get to a telephone. He needed to get in touch with Roger Hill. He needed to re-join the world.

The world needed to hear how Orson Welles pulled off the greatest prank in human history. He could push all other thoughts out of his mind.

# EPILOGUE

SATURDAY, NOVEMBER 6ᵀᴴ, 1938
7:08 PM EST
ITERATION ZERO
THE WHITE HOUSE
WASHINGTON, D.C.
EARTH, FOR THE FORESEEABLE FUTURE

It had been a busy week for Orson Welles. Roger Hill and John Houseman had worked together to get Orson back to Manhattan. Houseman neglected to ask any follow up questions about where he had disappeared to this time. On one hand, the fate of the woman could be determined easily enough. She would go down in the annals of Orson's personal history as just another ship that passed in the night.

His week of victory was not without its defeat. As the play featured no invading aliens to keep their attention, audience apathy would quickly doom *Danton's Death* to an early close. The Blue Coal Corporation, not looking to court the least bit of controversy around its radio program, released Orson from his contract to play *The Shadow*.

None of it mattered.

The press conference after the hubbub surrounding the *War of the Worlds* broadcast went exceptionally well, with the footage taken at the event already playing in newsreels all across the country. Orson Welles was finally in the motion picture business, and he didn't need the telegram inviting him to Los Angeles from George Schaeffer, President of RKO Pictures, to confirm that reality.

An aide emerged from the curved door and headed for Orson and Houseman as they waited. "Excuse me, gentlemen?" the aide said, snapping Orson from his daze. "They'll see you now."

The room was meant to intimidate, being the official office of Franklin Delano Roosevelt. It did not disappoint. The man himself – the most powerful man in the country, although Orson may have been just a touch more famous at that particular instant – moved towards them. Mrs. Roosevelt stood just behind him.

Houseman gasped at the image of the President. The rumors about his wheelchair were true. Orson was not fazed by the President's method of travel in the slightest. Everyone had secrets they hid in plain sight.

"Now, you fellas shouldn't feel the need to stand on my account," Roosevelt said, shaking both men's hands. They in turn shook Mrs. Roosevelt's hand.

"Now, Franklin," the First Lady admonished him. She didn't sound too terribly different from how Houseman often addressed Orson. "You gentlemen will have to excuse him. His mother once told him he was funny, and he never had occasion to disagree with her."

The President grimaced in a manner that gave the two men permission to laugh at both remarks. "Now, you, sir are the man who managed to frighten all of America. How about that!"

"Well, parts of New Jersey, at any rate," Orson demurred. When asked — and the question had been incessant over the last week — he often displayed this false modesty. Even so, he would continue to grow the myth around the night of October 30th. It was only way to ensure that no one tried to find out the truth.

"Don't sell yourself short, young man," Roosevelt remarked. "I could use you with Congress."

They all laughed again, but in all truth, some element of politics did appeal to Orson. Roosevelt turned to Houseman. "And you are Mr. Welles' producer, is that right?

Houseman nodded, still not quite able to move past the President's chair. "Yes, sir. John Houseman."

"Ah, yes," Roosevelt said. He clearly already knew the name of anyone entering his inner sanctum. "Well, if you gentlemen would like a seat. We'll get some pictures."

The photographers exposed their film several times, after which the President leaned over to Houseman. "Now, Mr. Houseman, if you don't mind. I'm going to see if I can get a picture of just me and Mr. Welles. My grandchildren are very fond of his radio appearances, and I will look like something of a bigger shot than I am if it appears we're old chums."

Houseman smiled amiably, rose from his seat, and moved out of the photographer's shot. "Very good," Roosevelt encouraged him, and then called out for his aide. "Thomas, will you ensure Mr. Houseman is comfortable in the next room?"

Houseman was not in any position to question the decision. He would often ask Orson over the next several years what he and the President spoke about over the next few minutes, but Orson was never once tempted to tell him.

"You could stand to get rid of him," the President muttered *sotto voce* when Houseman was safely out of earshot.

"Believe me, I'm trying," Orson said conspiratorially. "You don't even know the half of it – he's a Republican."

Despite the lie, Roosevelt smiled. "Oh, dear."

Orson posed for another snap from the photographer, but it never came. Mrs. Roosevelt showed the photographer out of the room, closing the door behind him. "Now, Mr. Welles," she began firmly. "How did you manage to do it?"

Orson was at a loss for words. "Now, dear," the President said. "Don't scare the poor fellow."

"He shouldn't have anything to be frightened of, not with where he's been," the First Lady snapped back at her husband. "Honestly, Franklin, while I am more progressive in oh-so-many matters, do not think for one moment we should not utilize the very best weapons in pursuit of our values."

Roosevelt relented and gave silent permission for Orson to speak freely. "With all due respect, Mrs. Roosevelt, the less people know, the better off we all are."

The First Lady seemed supremely dissatisfied with that answer, while the President appeared to accept it. "That's all well and good, Mr. Welles, but I'm afraid there is one more question we need answered."

"And that is?"

"Where are the ships – that is, those ships that were at Grover's Mill?"

Orson hesitated only because he never thought he would have to answer this question. The first couple took his reticence as such. "We're no ordinary people, Mr. Welles," Mrs. Roosevelt assured him. "We have access to a great deal of information about that night. Did you not think we would find the more damaged craft?"

Orson found an answer. "The ships clashed in orbit. They're unlikely to return."

Mrs. Roosevelt was again dissatisfied, but her reaction was certainly more muted than before.

"Well, Mr. Welles, despite your cageyness, we can certainly put you to use," the President said.

"I beg your pardon?" Orson asked.

"Paranormal phenomena, Mr. Welles," Roosevelt explained. "You may be the most experienced man in these matters in all of American history. I frankly doubt this is the last time such circumstances will befall the Earth. We may need to call on you again to save the world."

Orson's whole life spread before him, and the sum of the experience was once again a total mystery.

"Yes," Mrs. Roosevelt begrudgingly agreed. "But you are a tad more famous than the normal operative. Isn't he, dear?"

Roosevelt nodded. "Quite right."

"He'll need a code name, a *nom de intrigue*," Mrs. Roosevelt said.

The President snapped his fingers. "I've got it!" he said. "I've got the perfect code name."

"We're all in perfect suspense, my love," Mrs. Roosevelt said.

"His first mission was during Hallowe'en. We'll call him the Jack-o'-lantern."

Orson went pale, but said nothing. Mrs. Roosevelt moaned in horror. "How about October?" she suggested.

"What do you think?" Roosevelt asked Orson, seemingly agreeable to the change. "Agent October?"

Orson remained speechless.

# ACKNOWLEDGMENTS

First, I would like to thank a few people that—had it not been for the planet's favorite dog—would have been in the dedication.

Thanks go to my parents, who first showed me *Citizen Kane*. I can't imagine they thought this would be the result.

Thanks also go to Nicholas Meyer, who mastered the Space Opera, the night that panicked America, H.G. Wells, and time travel long before I ever tried. We all toil in his shadow.

Beyond those initial entries, my search for the book I write entirely on my own proceeds apace. This, however, is far from that book. It has been an often difficult process sending the director of *Touch of Evil* to the fourth planet and bring him back, but as I near the end, I'm glad I didn't leave Welles on Mars and try to write something without multiple universes, repeated time travel, and the restraints of a prequel.

Thanks to my wife, Lora. She puts up with a lot, and is impressed by the amount of words I (think I) know. She is the first reader of all my writing and often the most encouraging.

Thanks also go to Drs. Bruns, Bell,* and Zukafkas, who managed to put me out of commission just long enough to get this book back on track.

Caroline Miller read an early version of the first few chapters, and provided infinitely useful feedback. The writer's group moderated by Steve Amos also patiently listened while I read early chapters aloud. Without them, the amount of references to rhubarb in this volume would be significantly less. Any instances of POV shifts are in open defiance of them. Matthew McSpadden also read a more recent version of the book, in an effort to see if the final product played together as one piece. Orson is 10% less of a sociopath in the story thanks to him. It was a necessary change. Matt's other thoughts proved invaluable as well.

The Nevermore Edits Group has been key in shaping the text you have presumably just finished. Adrean, Jack, Shannon, CJ (the other one), Brooks, Kaz, Samantha, Ryan, Malea, and Mike. I could call each of you out by name for the help you have given me this year, and I think I just did. To avoid info dump: The next one will have more dick in it, I swear**.

Thanks go to those in charge of the estate of Howard Koch for never getting back in touch with me. While Mr. Koch's contributions to *The War of The Worlds* cannot be diminished, moving away from a strict mimicking of the text of that broadcast made several moments of the book much better than I originally conceived them.

Bill Fisher persists in earning my undying gratitude for his improvements to my various projects. Once again, he produced a cover which is both uniquely tied to this story, and of a piece with his previous work on *The Devil Lives in Beverly Hills*. Frequent lunches with him at the Ocean China buffet restaurant during my brief adventure in Bartlesville helped me remember what Mac Boyle is supposed to be doing. Without those lunches, I might be still trapped in middle-management purgatory, and this novel may have remained a half-baked couple of chapters forever floundering in my archives.

And finally, an apology to George Lucas for anything I might have said in the last fifteen years. Prequels are tricky things. People shouldn't be so hard on you. Somehow, I'll find a way to make things right.

Now, on to the next book!

#theswordsurvives

~MB
Party Now Apocalypse Later HQ
November 2015

* There. Are you happy, Jack?

** It probably won't. Probably.

# ABOUT THE AUTHOR

MAC BOYLE is a writer. With Bill Fisher, he is the co-creator of "The Adventures of Really Good Man." He has made it his life's work to put the filmmaker Orson Welles in unusual situations. He is currently working on the third book in the series, where Welles will try to successfully run an Arby's franchise in Toad Suck, Arkansas*. In his spare time, Boyle works for an un-named federal agency that is one-hundred percent NOT a cover for the CIA. If the universe hadn't seen fit to create pinball, he might have been a truly great man. He lives in Oklahoma** with his wife, Lora.

Follow him on twitter: @partyapocalypse.

Read more at partyapocalypse.com.

* That started as a joke, but I'm worried it is now all-too real.

** Not to be braggy, or anything...

Made in the USA
San Bernardino, CA
01 September 2018